STANDING PART HIDDEN

Esther Naylor

For love and Justice.

Preface

There is no such thing as stereotypical behaviour when it comes to presenting as a rape victim.

Shaila Dewan, in an article titled, 'Why Women Can Take Years to Come Forward with Sexual Assault Allegations', writes, 'There is no one response to sexual assault. A trauma victim can easily appear, calm or flat, distraught or overtly angry.'

She also quotes Kimberly A. Lonsway, a psychologist, who conducts law enforcement training on sexual assaults, as the research director for End Violence Against Woman International. 'Offenders are more likely to choose victims who have previously been assaulted – but a woman who reports more than one assault, is less likely to be believed.'

Part One

1

Tully sat quietly in her bedroom, perched on the side of her queen-sized bed, thinking back, trying not to make a sound. He once told her that he could hear every word. That even her soft breath was audible. Dare she breathe?

Perched there, legs hanging loosely over the side, looking out at the double-storey houses with their lavish gardens, she wondered what had set her off; this ceaseless dialogue, this underlying vibration. If she hadn't been a writer she may have been more concerned. But where was it all heading?

Would she write it down? Turn it into some kind of story?

'The ramblings of a white woman.' She considered carefully. How would it go? Who would be her audience? Would it simply be a conversation between two, perhaps three people? Or would she elaborate, flesh it out. Include shocking and precise details of her life and her parents, Ben and Freda, who suffered so badly and who she missed, and at times found so hard to let go. Her experience had shattered her, but yet, had left her strangely strong.

She had tried hard to keep the emotion in, but it had begun trickling out, over the sides pouring, pouring down, flooding her.

She moved over to her computer.

Where to start? Tully considers, staring at her computer keyboard. How to start? She pulls her long-sleeved black t-shirt down over her wrist, over her knuckles, over her hands and begins carefully wiping the keys with it as if by cleaning them, they would miraculously oblige and produce the right letters, form the perfect words and create the perfect beginning.

She ponders the question. How did it all begin? Was it the high school where she was employed at the time? The gym she frequented? Was it one of the men she said hello to as she passed the gym on her way into the aerobics room? Did one of them misread her intention. She wondered how anyone could misconstrue a simple hello. Or was there somebody harbouring an ill-conceived grievance against her, some imagined blame, attributed to her, existing only in their sick minds. They had spread slander about her and declared it as fact. Had someone decided to take revenge for something she knew nothing about. She concluded that it could have been at either, the gym or the school. The common denominator? The ethnic group present at both.

Tully, is forty-two-years-old, with below shoulder length, blonde hair and one hundred and fifty-eight, point five centimetres tall without shoes on, not nearly as tall as she would have liked. She has always been interested in the Arts and while teaching, she was frequently involved in one creative pursuit or another; acting for instance, also taking on courses, to expand her professional experience. She was engaged in a course, which required a great deal of writing and realized how much she enjoyed it. So, she began to write short film scripts, one of which, she was developing into a feature film script.

At school she loved sport. Even managed to captain a house team. Never making it to the highest level did not worry her in the least. It was sport she loved. Most sports. Except of course if it involved danger, such as white water rafting or even skiing.

In the sports store, after much thought, she finally decided on a pair of running shoes. She had tried on so many, and found this particular brand best of all. They suited her arches. Unlike other runners, who usually had several pairs, she wore the same shoes until they wore out.

As soon as she put them on her feet she felt a surge of energy and the urge to run. The desire was always strong. All-encompassing. She wanted to sprint. She wanted to win. The times she didn't win, which were many, only made her more determined. There was something about the speed. She felt like she was achieving something special.

But when it came close to the sports day, and her school friends were on the track, training, she was nowhere to be seen. Still, Tully could and did sprint. Later on, when she was older, it was at the beach, on the hard sand, at the water's edge, where she did her sprinting.

She had always thrived on physical activity. Riding her friend's bicycle when she was at school and later on her own, all over town. Sometimes with her young daughter Rachael, sitting behind her in the child's seat, skinny, stark white legs suspended on either side. On one occasion they had pedalled off to Tully's singing lesson. They arrived and when Tully was in the middle of her vocal exercises, Rachael decided to sing her own song. The singing teacher was so taken with the child's confident nature and also by her singing style that he thought he would teach her instead. Although amused at that moment, Tully did not return to the class.

It was when her son Harry, was three years old that she decided to attend the gym and it was about then, and particularly after her divorce, the following year, that her life became more challenging.

When Harry was growing up, she kicked the football with him until her leg ached, played countless games of cricket with him, always expressing her wish that he curtails his passion for fast bowling, which she saw, if he veered off target, as the oncoming of a dangerous weapon. They often played with a tennis ball, rather than a cricket ball but on this occasion, he insisted on the cricket ball. She was extremely thankful for her padded armour.

'Throw it to me Mum!'

'Let me practise for moment. I'm just getting the hang of it. I'm used to a tennis ball remember!'

'You're not moving your arm properly. Watch,' he said as he demonstrated his bowling style. He had conscientiously watched the way his favourite cricket players bowled and had practised endlessly, at home, at school, and in the park.

'OK. I think I'll do better this time.'

Tully rotates her arm the way she has been shown and bowls.

Harry hits it on full.

'Good one!' she yelled, running for the ball.

Tully's belief nowadays is that she does her best thinking when on her treadmill at home, in the morning, still in her pyjamas. Her thoughts clear, precise and sequential. Taking heavy steps in her black running shoes. First the heel and then the toe. Zealously swinging her arms or bending them at the elbow, curving them upwards towards herself or swinging them from side to side across her body and then, punching, punching, punching it out. Decimating the invisible and not so invisible enemy.

2

The High School was a place Tully really liked to work. Good cohesive staff and nice students. Upon reflection she noted that there was one aspect of her teaching duties she could well have done without; that of supervising an after-school detention class, which was conducted in an extremely small, bare and unattractive room with a few chairs, a bench, a couple of desks and a telephone, in case of trouble. It was the last resort for students who had taken no notice of warnings, or conduct cards, persisting instead with disruptive behaviour.

The students were forbidden to engage in any activity what so ever, or to converse. A punishment, which proved to be very difficult for both students and supervising teachers.

One of the four boys in the detention room suddenly had a pocketknife in one hand and with it, was attempting to cut the other hand. Startled, Tully tried to stop him, but could not. In distress she picked up the telephone and rang the coordinator who quickly arrived and removed the boy from the group.

Following up on the boy's welfare, she was informed that his mother had been contacted. She had not seen him for a couple of weeks when their paths crossed one morning, in the school grounds, between classes. 'I haven't seen you for a while. Where have you been?' She asked him. He said 'My mother took me on a holiday interstate and the break from school was great because it gave me more time with her. And that was what I needed. Thanks.'

Pleased as she was with the outcome, Tully was glad that she did not need to take another class like that again. In fact, it was a few months after this, that she and her husband sold their inner suburban home and she moved, with her twelve-year-old son, into a rented apartment, in a very attractive suburb. Leaving that particular high school behind her. She wanted both children with her but sadly for Tully, Rachael moved with her father, into a three-bedroom home.

3

There is a prevailing buzz in the staff room at morning recess. People are sitting and standing around in groups, drinking tea and coffee, having exquisite leftovers from last night's meal, or rolls, cakes, discussing various topics, such as football, school excursions, other staff members, students and personal matters.

Tully, is dressed in smart casual clothes: black and grey tweed knee length skirt, black woollen jumper, black tights and black ankle boots. She makes her coffee and moves across to the far side of the room and sits down on the large brown, imitation leather couch, under the windows, next to a group of friends including Lily.

The bell, signifying the conclusion of recess, rings, and Tully's group prepare to leave for their classes. Tully picks up her books, folder, paper and pencils and makes her way out into the corridor and down the passage to her next class.

The students are streaming into the corridors, pushing, shoving, yelling, chewing, some whistling, a few already at their lockers quietly getting ready for their next class.

*

Tully's, students are sitting along a narrow-extended table, in a light but small room. She is standing in front of them, an English as a Second Language book, in hand. She begins reading a section from the book: Hugh, who had slept in as usual, was running late for school. He grabbed his school bag from the bedroom floor and two pieces of fruit from the fruit bowl in the kitchen, as he yelled, 'Bye Mum.' He hurried down the passage and out of the front door to the bus stop, which, luckily for Hugh, was outside his house. The bus was stationary. The bus driver seeing Hugh, called out, 'come on Hugh, hop on.'

A boy interjects. 'Miss, don't you buy stationery from the Post Office? How is the bus stationary?'

Tully explains that in English, there are words that sound the same but have different meanings. 'They are called HOMONYMS.' Her students, laugh attempting to pronounce the difficult word; Homonym.

'In this case,' continuing her explanation, the end of the word is spelt differently. Yes,' she says, 'stationery means writing paper, pens and pencils. And that,' she pauses for a moment, then begins writing the word on the board, 'is station ERY.' She underlines the ERY. 'But, in this case, the bus was no longer moving. It was standing still, which means it was stationary.' She writes stationary on the board, and underlines ARY.

'What does Hop on mean, Miss?' someone else asks. She says, 'Hop on here, is slang for, get on. The driver means, get on the bus Hugh. But this is also, to hop, hopping.' And she demonstrates, hopping on one leg, eliciting more hilarity.

4

Tully makes her way up the corridor, to her next class, which is an extra, carrying a large black shoulder bag, a folder, pencils and drawing paper. She stops at her classroom, unlocks the door and enters the room, placing all of her things on the front desk. She begins tidying up a little. Takes a blackboard duster out of the front desk drawer and cleans the blackboard.

Her students have lined up outside the room. She walks over to the door, indicating that they should enter. They file in. A boy casually drops a conduct card onto her desk. When everyone is seated, Tully commences her class. She tells them that she has brought in some drawing paper and pencils but that they can work on any subject during the period. Pointing to her desk she says, 'When you've finished the work you need to do, there are some crossword puzzles here.'

Many of the students request the puzzles. She takes a bundle out of the folder and distributes them, ensuring that every student has something constructive to do. She sits down to mark assignments but after approximately twenty minutes, with an escalating noise level, Tully ceases marking, confronted as she is, with an undesirable spectacle. Sheets of foolscap are being folded into paper planes and propelled out of the back windows, towards the sports class.

'Please close that window and go back to your desks. You've got enough to do.'

The students resume their seats and the class settles down.

Not knowing this particular group, Tully holds up the conduct card on her desk, 'Who gave me this?' She asks. One of the boys who had been artfully directing paper plane out of the back-window, responds. 'I did Miss. I've got nothing to do.'

'What about your crossword?'

'I can't be bothered. Nobody else is doing anything.'

'Yes, they are and you're on a conduct card. You're not meant to be messing around. I'm going to write exactly what you've been doing in class. So, you'd better do some work.' She pauses for a moment and walks over to his desk 'Let's see how you're going.' She picks up his scrappy sheet of paper. 'You can do more than that. What about all your homework. Why don't you do it now, so you don't have to at home.'

Tully returns to her desk. A girl asks for assistance completing her English homework and sits down to work with Tully. The room remains quiet for another fifteen minutes before pandemonium, once again, breaks out. At the back of the room four boys are crumpling paper into balls and aiming them into imaginary basketball rings. She stands up quickly, 'Return to your seats immediately. The four boys involved in this escapade, have a lunch time detention tomorrow. In this room.' The boys complain. 'Oh why?' 'What have I done?' 'I didn't do anything!'

She picks up her book and writes down their names. It includes Angus, the student on the conduct card. She says, pointing to the card, 'Angus, I have to fill this card in. What do you think I'm going to write when you're behaving like this? I've warned you already.'

He shrugs his shoulders.

The first bell rings and the class pack up and are dismissed.

Tully sits down at her desk to fill in the in the conduct card. Angus is standing behind her chair, looking over her shoulder. He reads aloud as Tully writes. 'Angus could have done more work this period...' He stops after the first sentence and says, 'Miss, if you say that, I'll get into really bad trouble at home.'

'You know I'm being fair. I warned you. I told you what I was going to write and I'm not going to lie.'

'Well' he says, 'excuse me Miss but you can get F....d'

5

It is lunch time during the school holidays. The city streets are bustling. Tully strides down the vibrant street towards Flinders Street Station wearing trendy casual clothes: black pants, black medium heels and a yellow blouse and carrying a large black shoulder bag.

The streets are filled with parents, prams and children, groups of youths, buskers and spruikers gesticulating, trying to attract the attention of those passing by. Tully is oblivious to the noise and walks quickly and purposefully to the train station. She buys a ticket and proceeds down the platform, stepping into a crowded carriage. She finds a seat. The train begins to move.

Rhythmic rocking, repetitive engine noise as Tully sits motionless in the rapidly moving, long silver train wondering what she was going to do. She was feeling lost and uncertain. How did she get into this situation? She had been married, had two beautiful children and living in the family home. There were problems in the marriage yes, but on the whole, she felt comfortable in the role of mother and wife. No not just comfortable. She loved being a mother and a wife. And here she was with nowhere to live and her possessions in storage.

For the time being she was staying with a friend but it was not really working out. Her friend was used to living on her own and Tully was used to having her own home. Her house had been sold and until she found somewhere to live, Harry was staying with his father and sister. Her canary yellow hatchback had broken down and she was travelling around on public transport.

Her mind wanders. Her son is five years old and they are both walking home after school. Harry is riding his bicycle and Tully is walking beside him carrying his school bag. He tells her that he threw his orange away at lunch time that day. 'Really you threw, your orange away?' 'Yes, I did,' he said. She said, 'You wasted a perfectly good orange?' 'Yes, I promise. I threw it out.' She asked him why. He replied, 'I don't know. I just couldn't carry it around anymore.' 'Well,' she said. 'It's lucky it wasn't organic.' They both laughed. Then he sped his bicycle up attempting to turn the front wheel from left to right then, right to left, imitating older BMX riders.

That night Tully lay beside Harry in bed as she usually did, reading to him and then she recited the last few lines of psalm 91.

'I will rescue those who love me.
I will protect those who trust in my name.
When they call to me, I will answer;
I will be with them in trouble.
I will rescue and honour them.
I will reward them with a long life
and give them my salvation.
AMEN.'

Harry said he liked that prayer and that it made him feel safe. She had agreed. It was a very reassuring prayer.

She got out of bed and tucked the loosely hanging sides of the blanket securely under his mattress, kissed him and said 'Goodnight, I love you honey bunch.'

He smiled, 'Love you more. Goodnight Mum.'

Tully left the room and walked slowly, clomping noisily, down the passage, turned and crept quickly back to his bedroom. Poked her head around the door, taking Harry by surprise.

'Love you most!'

Harry burst into laughter.

She wandered into the loungeroom and sat back on the couch, picked up her Vogue magazine and carelessly thumbed through it. She heard movement in the passage, looked up and saw Harry in his light-yellow, flannelette pyjamas hopping past the door, giggling. She laughed and called out 'Go back to bed Harry!'

6

Tully was jolted back into the present by the train stopping at a station. Passengers get on and off. Three young boys about twelve years old enter the carriage and look around for somewhere to sit. One of them sees Tully and says, 'Hey, that looks like Harry's Mum.'

Harry turned around. Her heart melted. He looked warm and soft, beautiful, surprised and emotional and really pleased to see her. He was wearing his light green check flannelette shirt, which was very fashionable for kids of that age, over the top of a brown tee shirt, a pair of black cotton pants with side pockets and some basketball sneakers. His light brown shiny hair combed to the side, falling across his forehead. She stared at him and wondered if he would come over and sit with her.

He came over and sat down next to her, put his head on her shoulder, looked up, and said 'Mum.' She put her arms around him and kissed him. 'Oh hi, Harry' she said. They sat very close. She held on to him. She hadn't seen him for about a week and had missed him very much.

'Where are you going'? she asked.

He said, 'To Chris's place.'

She told him that she was going to inspect an apartment and they chatted a little, other passengers casually glancing over at them, as they spoke. And then, just as suddenly they were saying goodbye. She watched him get off the train. He waved to her from the platform. And she waved back, from the window, until he was gone.

Harry's father wanted Harry to stay with him permanently and that did not help at all. He came home from work at seven o'clock at night. What was Harry supposed to do until then? The very idea terrified her. She knew her son wanted to be with his father and that he was torn. There was his loyalty toward her and the need for his father, plus the happy go lucky life he had there, his sister and many of his friends around him. Why would he want to live in an apartment?

The transition from primary school to high school had been a difficult one. He had come from a school which leaned more towards an alternative education, into a traditional high school, so even sitting at his desk for long periods of time required a lot of getting used to. He was a beautiful happy loving soul, always energetic and full of fun with an uncanny ability to see beyond the surface. He seemed to really notice things about people. For instance, when he was seven, he had wheeled his bike in through the open front door and down the passage, stopping next to Tully. She had introduced him to a man, Peter, who was there to fix the roof of their old Edwardian house. Peter said, 'I'll have to come back and spend a bit more time looking around in the roof. And then I'll be able to give you a more accurate quote.' And later, Harry said, he thought the man was creepy and asked her if she'd noticed, that he smiled with his lips but his eyes were cold and she said, 'Well maybe I won't get him to fix our roof, after all.'

He had not been doing at all well at school, while living at his father's house and never did any of his homework. He was totally unsettled and she believed that in terms of his school work he would be better off living with her. As it turned out she was right.

She got off the train and began walking up the steep winding road which led to her next house inspection. This time, she found an apartment on the first-floor, in a block, built in the nineteen sixties. It was located at the top of a hill, in a street edged with elegant, ancient, leafy trees, coincidently the same suburb in which she grew up. Not only that, it was one street away from her childhood home.

A memory surfaces. Tully, aged ten, in grade five, at Primary school. She is walking home from school, with a friend from class. They cross the busy road and walk into a narrow street, with parked cars on either side of the road, parallel to the main road. They turn into a short laneway which opens up into a wide street with houses, surrounded by well-maintained gardens.

As they entered the laneway they noticed, up ahead, a large group of students from their school following a slightly older girl who she did not recognize. The group were yelling abuse at the girl, ridiculing her, snickering, deriding, calling her vulgar names. She was clearly distressed, occasionally turning towards them, beseeching them to go away and to leave her alone.

Tully, was shocked. She had never encountered that kind of behaviour. As they were some paces behind, her friend said, 'Quick, let's catch up.' She asked, 'Why?' Her friend replied, 'So that we can join in.' 'No. I'm not going to join in.' 'Alright, we won't,' her friend said.

When they passed the gang, she asked her friend if she really would have joined in. 'No, not really.' But the fact is, Tully knew her friend would have joined in, if she had said yes. She had changed the mind and actions of her friend. In a positive way.

She had asked her friend who the girl was and why the gang were following her and behaving so nastily towards her. She had done nothing to them and was probably on her way home from school, as were they. Her friend, who knew many of the students in the gang, responded, that they thought there was something wrong with the girl, that she was 'mad'.

Looking back, Tully, wished she had, as a ten-year-old girl, the courage to have said something to the group. She thought, 'I hope my children never do that to anyone.'

Children can be extremely cruel, and responsible parents are their best guide. People do not normally follow others around the street, attacking them verbally, just because they seem different. Are we pack animals, preying on weaker, more vulnerable individuals? Isn't ours a civilized society?

Tully wondered how life turned out for the girl. But who would have thought, not Tully, not even in her wildest dreams, that years later, she would be the object of ridicule, abuse and injustice.

In her life as an Art Teacher, she endeavoured to teach a class on bullying, discussing with her students' various kinds of bullying and the destructive nature of it. She asked them to put themselves in the position of the bullied person. What would it feel like? Their task was to draw or paint their interpretation and engendering emotions of those potentially damaging situations.

*

The apartment was a very sunny place. Views of the city were visible from every window. It was surrounded by a few old elm trees and overlooked the neighbor's colorful, well-established garden, which included roses, her favorite flower.

The place had two balconies, a small but practical kitchen, a reasonable sized lounge room where they could fit most of their furniture and two bedrooms. Tully thought it was adequate, although she did have to sell quite a few items of furniture, in order to move in. But her favorite carved antique oak cupboard, with engraved ornate copper handles and Harry's new bike, which they left downstairs in the garage, were both stolen. She had her suspicions about who took the bike but they were only suspicions.

Once the lease to the apartment had been signed they had to wait a further two weeks before they could move in, so Tully bought a couple of tickets to Queensland to stay with her parents, who had retired to Broadbeach. It would give her time to breathe, a break from her life.

7

It was a sunny Queensland day as Tully and Harry along with a full aircraft load of passengers, carrying various bags, hats and other summery items, descended the aircraft passenger stairs. They walked across the tarmac and poured into the crowded Coolangatta Airport lounge, where Tully's parents, Ben and Freda were waiting. Seeing Tully and Harry in the incoming crowd, they waved excitedly and manoeuvred forward with enthusiastic greetings.

The family, laden with luggage; a huge, heavy, navy-blue suitcase, boogie board and a smaller brown bag, proceed through the airport and out into the airport car park. They load their luggage into the boot of Ben's white sedan, then pile into the car. Strap on their seat belts and drive out onto the busy Queensland highway. Ben and Freda in the front seat, Harry and Tully in the back.

Suddenly, Ben accelerates. Amazed he says 'Look!'

'At what?' Harry asks.

'The man on the bike. He's got a swastika on his jacket.'

'Stop it Ben. Don't get so agitated,' Freda says.

'You cannot drive around with a swastika. He must be a Nazi.'

They pull up at the light. Ben unlocks his door.

'No Ben. Leave him alone. Don't confront him.'

Ben jumps out of the car.

'Take your jacket off!' he yells at the motorbike rider.

'What?' the rider asks, incredulous.

'Take that jacket off. You are wearing a Nazi swastika. Millions of people were murdered under that sign. Take it off or I'll drive into your bike.'

The motorbike rider stares at Ben, then, removes his jacket.

'You are mad,' he says.

Ben gets back into the car.

Freda says, 'Ben, what's the matter with you? *'Bist du faruked tze vus?'* 'Are you crazy or what? You have to think before you do something like that. Do you know him? Do you know how he'll react?'

Ben does not answer.

Some time prior to this, Ben had walked past a bookshop in Surfers Paradise. Surfers Paradise, has many fashionable shops and cafés. It is always active, always crowded with buskers, street acts and loud music. Diversely dressed people, sitting inside and outside café's drinking and eating, young and old, tourists and locals, out for the day, seeing and being seen. He noticed a book written by a well-known Holocaust denier, displayed in the front window of the book store. Enraged, he went into the store and demanded that the they remove the book immediately, telling them that he had lived through the Holocaust in Europe and assured them that it did happen. The bookstore removed the book from view. He passed the bookshop many times after that incident. The book was no longer displayed.

8

It was unfortunate that when Tully and Harry, returned to Melbourne from Queensland and went to their new apartment, the carpet, which must only have been washed that afternoon, was still wet. Their furniture was due to arrive the following day and so the place was bare and unwelcoming.

Harry took one look at the empty, soggy apartment and was about to cry. She could tell he was wishing he was back at his father's warm house. He told her that he didn't want to be there and asked why he couldn't live with his father. And her heart ached for him and for herself. She really should have waited until she had moved in properly so that he could have walked into something more welcoming, a place which felt like home. Not this. But it was too late now and they had to make the most of it.

She tried to reassure him that it would all work out for them and in desperation, said 'I'll get you a dog as well,' knowing that he longed for one. Although, she did not know if they were allowed to keep a dog in the apartment.

Tully hung Harry's school uniform in one of the cupboards and put the bag of food she had brought with her, on the kitchen bench. They had no beds to sleep in but they did have their bedding; blankets, sheets, doonas and pillows. So, with Harry's reluctant help, they placed two large green garbage bags next to each other on the carpet, put a blanket on top of them and sheets on top of that.

Later, they lay down back to back on the blanket, wrapped themselves in their doonas and tried to go to sleep. Tully turned towards Harry and put her arm around him. She said, 'Harry'

'Mm.'

'I'm sorry I put you though this.'

The cold was coming up through the floor and she wished it was morning.

*

After breakfast the next morning, Tully gave Harry his lunch money and bus fare to get home. As she drove him to school, she pointed out the location of the bus stop, which fortunately was at the bottom of their steep street, exactly where the shopping centre began. There was also a bus stop directly outside the school building, so she knew that he would be able to get home easily. After dropping Harry off at school, she returned home and waited for their furniture to arrive.

That afternoon when Harry came home from school, his face shone as he looked into the apartment through the open front door. He was delighted to see that the apartment had been partially set up. He entered and headed straight for his bedroom, sat on his bed, bounced on it a few times, then leapt over to the giant full-length poster of his favourite basketball player, which was pinned to the wall. He measured himself up against it and said, 'Hey Mum, look! I think I've grown. Do you?'

Tully moved closer to Harry, 'Of course. You must have grown. It's been about a month hasn't it? Look how tall you are.' Pointing to the poster, she said, 'You'll be as tall as him pretty soon. What about me.' Wishing she could have been taller and standing on tiptoes against the poster, stretching herself way beyond her natural height, she asked, 'Have I grown?'

'You? You're not going to grow. You're just a shrimp.'

Tully messes his hair and gives him a playful push out of the room.

*

When Tully and Harry set off to school, the first morning after sleeping in the new apartment, they were quite unaware of the delivery van parked down the street a little way off. Neither did they notice the two men sitting inside the van watching them leave. Nor the dark blue Mercedes Benz parked, behind it.

9

Steven and Peter, wearing identical outfits, blue basketball hats and orange jackets, emerge from their van and surreptitiously scan the street before nonchalantly, sauntering over to Tully's apartment. Steven is wearing a pair of expensive brown leather loafers which, are completely incongruous with his workman's outfit. He hangs around the entrance to the apartment, while Peter runs upstairs, two at a time. In his haste he slips on the top step. He mouths an expletive, regained his balance and instantly begins fiddling with the front door lock. He appears edgy and works quickly, opening the door with brazen efficiency. He enters the apartment. Shoves his hands into his pockets and pulls out some bugging devices, which he carefully places in strategic positions around the apartment. They are tiny. He glances back around the room as he closes the front door behind him. He runs downstairs. 'How'd it go?' Steven asks.

'Piece of cake!'

At that moment, a woman residing in the apartment block, dressed in a navy-blue suit, navy high heels and carrying a red patent leather bag, comes walking brusquely down the path. She is on her way to work. As she approaches, Steven busies himself pretending to examine the taps, both hands twisting.

He smiled beguilingly at her, 'Good morning, nice day.'

'Good morning,' she replied, noticing his shoes. Unperturbed, he charmingly displayed his even, white teeth.

*

The following morning Steven and Peter return to Tully's apartment in their delivery van. Standing on the nature strip Steven heedlessly slides the van's side door fully open and hands Peter a toolbox and some hosepipe. He takes the extension ladder out of the van, then closed the van door.

They carry their equipment over to the side of the apartment block and position the ladder up against the wall. Steven climbs up the ladder with the toolbox in his right hand. He places the toolbox on the roof and removes some of the tiles, leaving an open space. He calls down to Peter, 'Hand me the hose, will you?' Peter obliges. And Steven pushed the hose through the open space. Then, he climbs into the opening, with the toolbox.

He drills a few small holes into the ceiling. Pushes one end of the hose into a hole, leaving the other end hanging over the side of the building. He climbs back out of the roof and replaced the tiles. Takes a knife out of the toolbox and cuts the hanging part of the hose even with the tiles.

He climbs back down the ladder, carrying the toolbox and remaining hose.

Peter collects the ladder and he and Steven head back to the van, where they deposit their equipment. Peter noisily pulls the van door shut.

10

Cigarette smoke is wafting out of the van window. It is dark. Steven and Peter are sitting inside the van, smoking and listening to music. They look up at Tully's window. The light is still on. They wait. The light goes off.

Peter, who is carrying the extension ladder and Steven a sports bag, are both wearing earpieces. They sneak into the front garden, and quietly lean the ladder up against the wall. Steven quickly climbs up the ladder, clutching the bag, while Peter remains on the lookout.

Steven takes a small pump, containing an anaesthetic spray, out of his bag and inserts it into the hose. He begins pumping. Waits for a few moments, then repeats the action.

Peter said quietly 'Are they out to it yet?' Steven listens intently. 'Can't hear anything.' He hesitates. 'No, wait...' Then, 'I think we can move in now. Be very quiet.'

'This is called abuse and invasion of privacy.' Peter says smugly. Steven smiles back, 'Yes... Yes, it is. Lucky she won't remember any of it, isn't it?'

*

It is close to one o'clock in the morning. Tully is half asleep. She senses someone is in her room, close to her bed.

'Harry,' she murmurs.

Silence.

She can feel someone touching her but she can't move or speak.

'Shhhhh Jshhhhh Jshhhhhh Jshhhhhh,' she struggles to enunciate.

Faltering, Peter says, 'I'm not touching her.'

'I'll have to do it then.'

Steven sits on Tully's bed holding a syringe. She's asleep. He spikes her arm with drugs. She moans, 'Awww, you're hurting me.'

Arrogantly, he replies, 'Hold still then and I won't hurt you.'

Tully, is sprawled out on a double bed in a drug induced sleep. Steven and Peter are ransacking her bedroom. The cupboards and drawers are all open. They go through everything, touching, inspecting, marking and tearing her clothes.

Peter, ill at ease, bites his lip. He's forty-eight years old and taller than Steven. His appearance is generally rougher than his associates. He has a longish, face with visible cheekbones, though you could not call them prominent. His limp light brown hair falls below his unremarkable ears and he has a small even nose, so generally, he never stands out in a crowd.

He is a highly superstitious male, though he would not allow himself to give any thought to justice. Otherwise how could he do what he was doing? Right? He doesn't consider himself an unkind or bad person. He could be very considerate really. Doesn't he take his son to soccer practice every week and hang around to watch him play? He always takes the rubbish out. He's really just a regular guy with obligations. His family. No, it was his job and he had to do it. He had to make a living after all.

Steven pries into one of Tully's drawers and comes across some valuable jewellery, including a beautiful, large cameo broach. He scrutinizes each piece, extremely pleased with his find and stuffs them into his pockets. Then continues rummaging.

They both work quickly and obsessively, carefully returning each item to its original position.

Steven has an air of confidence about him. He's five foot eleven inches tall, fifty years old with black short well-cut hair, large brown eyes and an olive complexion, an aristocratic nose, his teeth are even and white and his smile broad. His earlobes are slightly elongated and he is usually well attired. He takes pride in his body, regularly working out at the gym. He sees himself as quite smooth.

He notices Tully's bag and rifles through it. Finds her purse and discovers two one hundred dollars notes, which he pockets. He replaces the money with two ten-dollar notes. He had it all he thought. Money, double storey house in a well-heeled area, took his family to Surfers Paradise every year. His wife adored him. She didn't have to go out to work and kept the house beautifully clean. His twelve-year-old son went to a private boy's school where he received an excellent education and his eight-year-old daughter happily attended a private girl's school. He wanted the best for his children. Even if it meant this. He looked down at Tully. Powerless.

Yes, of course he had to answer to others, but that was just part of it, part of life. The question of right or wrong never entered into it.

He had been told a bit about Tully. Not much. She was a teacher and Jewish. He didn't know any Jews. Where did they come from Israel or somewhere? Didn't they kill Jesus? Tight with money, too, weren't they? Although she didn't look like she had too much money to be tight with. Anyway, he preferred to stick to his own nationality. Strength in numbers. That was the key. There were a few Australians he was friendly with but usually they worked in the same field as he did. And some who had married into his culture.

Look, he had people working for him, Peter for instance. He might be smart. He didn't know how smart that was, but he was definitely not as smart as him. Peter was all right. They needed people like that. Mercenaries who will do anything for money. Good at his job and did what he was told. Steven and Peter were duplicitous, extremely nice to each other but careful.

Steven and Peter had broken into Tully's home with some deranged notion that they had the right to, were entitled to, drug and brutalise her. They had been paid. That gave them the right. She was of no consequence to them. Wasn't even of their ethnicity. Simply put they did not quibble about their work.

Steven notices Tully's computer sitting on the dresser. He walks over to it and boots it up. He locates Documents. Scrolls through, opening some of her files. Curious, Peter follows. He leans in.

*

They move over to her bed, lift her, and lay her down onto a blanket on the floor. Steven kneels next to Tully and opens a neat, black case. He removes a few surgical instruments and roughly, begins distorting Tully's face. He probes into her mouth and nose. The other watches.

Peter says, 'I don't even know why I'm doing this half the time.'

You're getting paid for it. That's why.'

Tully yells, 'J-E-S-U-S!'

Peter begins trembling. Stepping back, he says, 'I don't want to go on with this right now. She's calling Jesus.'

'So, what! Nothing happens. Hold her mouth open will you.' He waits for a second or two. 'Open it wider will you!' Automaton like, Peter responds.

'We'll chip away at her yet.'

Finally, he injects fluid into her nose and carefully packs up his case. And so, the process of rearrangement begins.

Suddenly feeling courageous, Peter gets under the doona and attempts to force himself onto Tully.

'I wonder if I can get her to have sex with me?' he says.

'I'm sure you can. Just tell her it's someone she knows.'

Tearing at her pyjamas cord, Peter says in frustration, 'I can't get it off.'

'Just rip it off!'

Tully, pushes him away. 'What are you doing? Get off. Get away. Get away from me!'

Peter says, 'It's your husband honey... I'm going away, I need to get close to you before I go.' Clammy hands groping.

'Get out. Get out. GET OUT!' Tully yells, arms wildly flailing.

'You'd better get off or you'll wake her son.'

'Don't worry. I'll get her tomorrow night.'

Unpleasantly, Peter says, 'Good job. Not so pretty now is she.'

'Nah,' Steven replies. 'Let Jesus help her!'

They laugh, flick off the light and leave the room. The door snaps shut.

11

Tully is driving a modern grey sports car with the hood on. The seats are very low and she doesn't reach the windows, so she is unable to see outside. She drives anxiously, hands gripping the steering wheel. The gloomy streets are deserted.

She stops her car on a kerb and opens her door. Three men are standing at the edge of the footpath looking straight ahead. Their heads and bodies are completely covered with long grey hooded robes. Only their eyes are visible. In despair she cries out, 'Help, help me! I can't see where I'm going.'

The three men do not respond. She stares at them. Horrified, she realizes that what she thought were eyes, were just empty black spaces. She wakes up.

*

In the morning, feeling quite groggy, Tully rolls across the bed and notices blood on her sheets. Dismayed, she runs her hand over the marks and groans, 'Oh God. I need help.' She peels off the quilted eiderdown and checks her arms, legs and t-shirt. Then gets out of bed and stares at the marked sheets. She rips them off her bed. Rushes into the bathroom and dumps them all into the clothesbasket. She feels sick.

Tully makes her way into the kitchen and puts the jug on, takes two slices of bread and puts them into the toaster, gets a teaspoon from the drawer, scoops coffee into her large white mug, which is on the bench next to the coffee jar. She rushes back into the bathroom, seizing the rack hanging, bath towel and catching sight of herself in the bathroom mirror. Gasps. There's blood in her hair and her face looks distorted.

Her usually rubicund, taut skin, is drooping down over her jawline: as though fat and tissue had been sucked out. Drained. Drained out of her now skeletal face. She felt like the dark plum red blood, had been leached from her veins. Probably filling small delicate jars somewhere, she thought, with gold or silver screw on lids. Or possibly, with little whitish plastic, screw lids, carefully held upright, ensuring, no spillage. Her nose was enlarged. A bulbous mass.

She examines her hair carefully using her fingers to part it into sections, trying to see where the blood is coming from.

In disbelief she covers her face with her hands. Removes them, staring at the damage. 'OH GOD!' She frantically rubs, scratches and scraps her face trying to make it look normal, washes it, then hurriedly dries it, pushing it this way and that, trying to balance it out. Trying to realign it. She opens the bathroom cabinet, takes out some makeup and lipstick. Plasters the makeup all over her face, then applies the lipstick. She replaces the cosmetics, brushes her hair and returns to the kitchen.

'Mum!' Harry yells from his bedroom.

She quickly pulls herself together. 'Yes?'

'Come in, it's Saturday.'

'OK. I'm just making myself a coffee.'

Tully opens the fridge, takes out the butter, vegemite and a bottle of orange juice and puts them on the bench next to the toaster. Then, she gets a tray, knife, glass and plate, puts the toast onto the plate, butters it and smears it with vegemite.

She fills the glass with orange juice, finishes making her coffee, puts everything on the tray and takes it into Harry's room.

'Good morning,' she says cheerfully, entering his room. She places the tray on Harry's bedside table. He sits up in bed, 'Hi Mum, hop in. Have your coffee here.' Harry makes a space for her next to him. She sits down, drawing the doona up over her legs, then kisses him and hands him the orange juice and toast. 'Here you are.'

'Thanks,' he says.

She takes her cup of coffee, sipping it slowly, becoming aware that Harry is scrutinizing her. She composes herself.

'What's happened to you?' he asks

'What time is Jack coming to pick you up?'

'Stop trying to change the subject. I hate it when you do that. I can see there's something wrong.'

'I'm just feeling very tired Harry.'

'Are you sure that's all it is?'

She hated lying to him, but it was not possible to tell him the truth.

'Yes,' she said.

'Well you can have a good rest today then.'

She smiled, 'I will.'

12

It was just before eleven o'clock in the morning, almost time for Harry's basketball game to commence. Tully was sitting in the front seat of her car, feeling poorly. She wanted to stay in there until the game began.

Harry was in the school grounds talking to other team members. His friends began moving into the basketball courts but he hung behind, waiting for Tully. He opened the car door and asked her if she was coming in to watch the game. She said, 'Yes, I am. But just let me sit here for a few minutes.'

'We have to go. The games about to start.'

She does not move. 'Alright.'

'Are you coming in to watch me?' he urges.

'I am coming in Harry. I'll be there to watch you even if I have to crawl in.'

There in the distance, to the far right, next to a taller man in the smart dark suit, the two deviants, Steven and Peter hang about smoking. Peter drops his cigarette and grinds it into the dirt with his shoe.

*

Ten thirty at night, Steven and Peter arrived at a suburban house. The door was opened by a male in his early fifties. He asks them both in and leads them into the lounge room where they are invited to sit.

The sideboard is covered with many family photos and pictures of children at various stages of development.

In the background a woman fills small wine glasses with ouzo. She takes the filled glasses over to her visitors.

The host opens his computer and adjusts the screen. They all watch.

Sitting on the side of the bed, in the dark, facing the bed head, Tully takes her night t-shirt and pulls it over her head covering her jumper. She undoes her bra strap from behind and slides one strap off her arm, together with the sleeve of her jumper, pulls them up over her head, and through the other arm and puts her night t-shirt on so that nothing can be seen.

The host raises his glass in a toast.

*

The next morning, Tully, enters the bath room and flings two matching pink bath towels over the shower screen. She steps into the shower wearing an oversized white t-shirt and a pair of long patterned pyjamas and slides the shower door closed behind her. She runs the water.

Emerging from the shower, dripping, one towel wrapped around herself, underneath the sopping t-shirt, she places the other towel over her head. It hangs over her shoulders. She sits down on the bathroom chair, bath mat under her feet. Very carefully, Tully removes the clinging pyjama pants and top and guardedly attempts to dry herself and get dressed. All under the towel.

Steven and Peter's eyes are fixed on the computer screen.

Steven says, 'Did you see anything?'

'Nah, ya won't.'

13

Although, things were moving along nicely for Harry, he was learning to play the guitar, doing a good deal of sport, some of his homework and generally improving at school, there were a few things that did concern Tully, beginning with the strange noises on her bedroom balcony the night before. She sat up in bed, listening. Then, got out of bed and peered through the venation blinds but could not see anything. She had groaned, and gone back to bed. And when she went out to look in the morning, she found cigarette butts. Neither she nor Harry smoked. She picked the butts up and carefully examined them, then checked the locks.

There were also strange noises on the roof at night, things went missing, including valuable jewellery. Her clothes had also been interfered with. At that precise moment, Harry called from his bedroom. She instantly dropped the butts and moved quickly, back indoors.

*

One morning, Tully was getting ready for work and looked in her cupboards for something to wear. She selected a plain dress but after noticing a few stains on it, she lay it down on the bed and continued her search. She found some black pants and a patterned top. She was about to take them into the bathroom when she saw that they too were stained and the top was torn. She examined them carefully finding it very puzzling because she did not remember tearing the top and she did not put stained clothes back into her cupboard.

She decided to go through each item in her wardrobe, finally, choosing a floral knee length skirt and a black, long sleeved t-shirt. She was about to carry her clothes into the bathroom but noticed some unusually dark marks on the bedroom door. She hesitates, perplexed, 'Oh.'

She continued into the bathroom and placed her clothes onto a chair, then opened a cabinet and removed some plastic gloves, a bottle of bleach and some CHUX. She put on some rubber gloves. Soaked the CHUX in bleach and set the bottle back down inside the cabinet. She returned to her bedroom and vigorously cleaned the door.

Still puzzled, Tully returned to the bathroom dropped the CHUX into a plastic lined rubbish bin. Removed her gloves, throwing them into the bin as well. She knotted the plastic lining. Then washed her hands, thoroughly.

It was obvious to Tully that someone, someone underhandedly, without her permission, was coming into their home. It horrified her. They had just moved in. She did plan to go to the Police. But telling Harry was never an option. The thought never even crossed her mind. He was entitled to a decent childhood and she was determined that he had one. It was her duty as a parent. And if, at the time, she believed that he was in any danger, she would never have allowed him to stay in the house. In retrospect, she can see that he could well have been in danger. What if he'd woken up and wandered into her room. What would have happened then? What would they have done?

But if Harry had picked up anything, and she thought there must have been times when he wondered what was going on with his mother, well he wasn't saying. So later, when he, as an adult, he told her that he had thoroughly enjoyed his childhood, that it had been great, it had moved her deeply.

She actually believed, naively, that she could handle the whole situation on her own. Of course, with help from the police.

14

Two o'clock in the morning, Tully dials 000.

'Police,' she says urgently.

'One moment please.'

She waits, nervously, listening to heavy treading on the roof above her.

'Police.' Speaking rapidly, Tully whispers, 'There's someone on my roof.'

'What's your name please?' the receptionist asks calmly.

'Tully Edwards.'

'Your address?'

She tells them her address. 'Please hurry,' she says frantically. 'The noises are really loud.'

Still calm, the receptionist says, 'Have you heard these noises before?'

'Yes. But this time they're really loud. Please hurry, there's someone up there, I'm sure of it.'

'We'll send somebody out as soon as possible.'

The clamour suddenly amplifies, then stops abruptly.

Tully puts the mobile down and half runs into her bedroom, where she throws on her dressing gown. She walks through to Harry's room and finds him sleeping peacefully. So, returns to the loungeroom and anxiously waits for the Police to arrive.

She hears the police car pull up outside and immediately opens the front door. Two Police Officers, both six feet tall, or thereabouts, appear in the doorway, one of them is holding a flash light, the other, a dark coloured book.

She blurts out, 'There was someone in or on my roof. I'm sure of it.'

Unruffled, one of the Police officers says, 'Do you have a man hole in the ceiling?'

'Yes, in the bathroom.'

She directed them both to the bathroom and hands the slightly shorter officer, a small, grey stepladder. He leans it against the wall and climbs up. Pushing the manhole cover aside, he peers into the dark roof, flashing his torch.

The taller officer, places the dark book onto the floor beside him, holds the step ladder ensuring its stability, while he and Tully wait in silence, occasionally looking up.

'Well there's no one in there now. If there was someone, they've gone.' He carefully steps down the ladder.

Disappointed, Tully says, 'The low-lives. They must've taken off when they heard me calling the police.'

'Has this happened before?' the shorter one asks, while the taller, scrutinizes her lounge room, inspecting personal articles and photographs.

'I've heard noises but they haven't been as loud as this before. What can you do about all this?'

'Not much. We don't have the funds... unless we know who the offenders are.'

The taller officer opens his book. 'I'll take down some details.'

*

Sometime later, she made an appointment to talk to a social worker whose office was close by. But she did not stay the whole hour. 'A social worker? Why didn't you go to the police?' Lily had asked.

'Well of course I went to the police in the first place. It's a police matter isn't it? But they said they didn't have the funds to deal with it. I thought, if I told the social worker, he might be able to get the police to help me. But after talking to him for a few minutes, I left because I realised it was a mistake going to see him at all.'

15

Riccardo, the social worker, came knocking on her door at lunch time in April during the first term school holidays. Tully was at home with Harry, Harry's friend and his friend's mother. They had come over mid-morning and the four of them were getting ready to go out for the day. She opened the door to see the social worker, standing there. An arrogant, dusty, shabby little man, haphazardly dressed. He was with another man who was taller, thinner and carrying a dark briefcase. His appearance was neater. She noticed that he had black hair and a relatively trendy haircut. She was sickened by the sight of them, there in the doorway of her apartment.

'Hello Tully, I've come to see you,' he grinned.

'You've come to see me? Why?'

He had the nerve to come to her home knowing that her child would be there and had actually brought someone else with him, to take notes, she imagined, at lunch time, during the school holidays.

'Ricardo,' she said. 'How dare you come here! I want you to leave'.

Riccardo turned to his friend and said, 'See how she is?'

'Yes,' he responded.

She shut the door.

'Promise me that you'll make another appointment to see me,' he had said, before she left his office.

'No, I won't promise, I can't promise because I won't be making another appointment,' she replied.

So, he had decided to go and see her instead.

He began harassing her. Ringing her, threatening her, getting in touch with child welfare, sending people to assess her, getting others to ring her, wanting her to make another appointment. He seemed convinced that she needed to see him. He had come to the apartment another morning when she was singing loudly to the radio and washing the dishes. But this time she did not open the door. She heard the knocking and simply held her breath. How did she know it was him? Intuition.

After a few minutes, she looked out of her first-floor window and saw him standing on the footpath talking to someone he had brought with him, possibly the same man. She wasn't sure. Her car was parked in the garage so he could have assumed that she was at home. That was the day her son's new bike was stolen.

'Are you saying he had something to do with that?' asked a doctor she had gone to see sometime later, to discuss Riccardo's visit. She knew Riccardo wanted to have her assessed so she decided to go and see a doctor of her own choosing.

'No, I'm not accusing anyone but that was the day it was stolen.'

'Coincidence?'

'Possibly.'

She had asked the doctor what she could do about the social worker and then the other, more frightening activities around her home. She needed help. He said he would help her. But when she asked him how he was going to do that, he raised both of his arms into the air slightly and said, 'You've just answered your own question.' A strange way of indicating his inability to help, she thought. And also, not at all encouraging. But as she was leaving his rooms, he exclaimed, 'You do not have to see the social worker Tully. This is not Nazi Germany.'

Thankfully, the doctor rang the harassing social worker and told him to stop bothering Tully. So that was the last she heard from that dusty little man. But he had already contacted Child Welfare and they turned up at Harry's High School unexpectedly and dragged him out of a Maths class while a test was in progress. They took him into the Principals office and asked him a number of questions. Harry's answers obviously satisfied them, because they contacted Tully the next day and quite casually, told her that they were not taking this case any further as Harry seemed quite happy.

But the effect had been profound on both Tully and Harry. She could feel her anger building inside her as she thought about it. She only found out when her son came home from school and said, 'Mum a man and woman came to school to talk to me today.'

'What do you mean?' she said, 'To the class?'

'No, they came to talk to me. We were doing a Maths test and they walked in with the Principal and said, "Harry come with us."

'We went into Mr. Clancy's office and they asked me a lot of questions.'

She sat down next to him.

'How horrible for you. What did you think when that happened, were you scared?'

'I was a bit,' he said.

'So, what did you do?'

He said, 'Nothing, I just answered them.'

'What kind of questions were they?'

'The man said, you're living with your mother at the moment aren't you Harry?'

'I said yes. And then he asked me how that was going.'

'What did you say?' Tully asked.

'Good. Then he asked me if I liked living with you and I told him I did. He asked, why was I living with Dad a little while ago and I told him that you were looking for a new apartment for us. Then the woman asked me if you were a good mother and if I loved you.'

'And?'

'I said a very good mother and I love you.'

They both laughed.

'Then she asked me if I loved Dad and was he a good Dad and who did I love most you, or him. And who did I like living with most you, or Dad. I said I loved you both and I liked living with both of you.'

Tully found it extremely difficult to believe that professionals dealing with young people could be so insensitive. She thought, three adults; the principal and two child welfare workers, marching into a maths class and in front of the entire class, asking Harry to come with them.

Harry's Maths teacher rang Tully afterwards to say how surprised and sorry she was and that she wasn't able to do anything about the situation. Tully appreciated her call.

That day after school she told Harry that Child Welfare had rung and they were going to stop bothering them from this point onwards. She went into his room, grabbed the football, threw it up into the air a few times, clapping her hands in between each throw, and said,

'Who's for a game?'

In the garden, Harry kicked the ball high, high into the air. Tully watched him run towards it, arms outstretched, looking up, getting ready for that perfect mark.

She waited for the right moment. Then moved in.

She elbowed him in the side, edging him out of the way. He elbowed her back. They laughed pushing each other about, competing for the ball.

16

Harry, now in year eight and thirteen years old, is in an English class where there is a photo of 'Piss Christ' on a screen at the front of the classroom. The photograph, which is a of a plastic crucifix submerged in a glass container of urine and blood, was created by the artist Andre Serrano, a devout Catholic.

The English teacher Mrs. Silver has been discussing the photograph with the class and has organized a debate for the following morning. The aim of the debate was to determine whether or not the artist ought to have created this controversial piece, which was protested against by various members of the public.

Harry, was sitting towards the back of the room talking with his friend Sean, when Mrs. Silver said, 'What have you got to say, Harry?'

'I was just talking about "Piss Christ", Mrs. Silver.'

She points to the front desk and says, 'Come up here Harry and bring your books.'

Harry and Sean give each other a 'Here we go,' look as he collects his books and carries them to the front table.

'The debate will be third and fourth period tomorrow. I expect everyone to be well prepared,' she says.

Dale, a boy sitting at the table behind Harry makes an ill-considered remark to him. Harry turns around to respond.

'That includes you Harry.' Mrs. Silver says.

The boy sitting next to Harry, playfully nudges him and laughs. Harry laughs and returns the nudge.

Mrs. Silver asks the class if there are any questions before they leave. Nobody puts their hand up. The lunch bell has rung. Finally, she says, 'Do your best and I'll see you all tomorrow.' The students hastily grab their books and rush towards the door. It's lunch time.

*

Tully sat on her double bed, propped up against the back wall, white pillows behind her, sewing the hem of a dress. Something she did when fashion changed the length of a dress or skirt. Harry, settled cross-legged, his elbows resting on his knees, was opposite her, his exercise book lying open on the bed in front of him.

He said, 'I'll have to do a good job on this, or Mrs. Silver will never let me hear the end of it.'

'What do you mean?' Tully said, 'She's a fabulous teacher. She said she really liked you, at parent teacher night.'

'Yeah, that's what she tells you. In class it's a different story,' he says, 'Anyway the debate's tomorrow and I have to write a paragraph about "Piss Christ".'

'What side are you on, for or against?'

'Against.'

'Did you choose that side?'

'No, the teacher told everyone the side they had to go on.'

'This is what we wrote in class.' He picked up his exercise book and began reading. 'Andrea Serrano, a devout Catholic was born in 1950. His photograph, "Piss Christ" is of a plastic crucifix submerged in a glass container of the artists own urine and some cow's blood.' He looked up for a moment to gauge Tully's reaction.

'Then, it says, how it caused a lot of outrage and violence at the Victorian National Gallery. Doors were closed to protect the Gallery and staff. And how two boys came to Melbourne from Sydney to smash the photo with a hammer.'

'You know, I've seen that photo and the red and gold colours are amazingly beautiful.'

'Are they? So, do you think it should've been banned?' he asked.

'I don't know about banning it Harry. That's censorship. What about the artists right to free expression? I'll take the other side.'

She put her sewing down beside her on the bed. 'You know Harry, throughout history, anything new or different in Art is initially considered to be shocking. Then, after a while, people begin to accept it and it becomes mainstream. Art is a visual language, it challenges and breaks down boundaries.' She waits for a moment. 'Do you think artists should censor their own work so as not to offend anyone?

'No, not really,' he answers. 'But what do you mean by a visual language?'

'Well, English is a verbal and written language, isn't it? When you want to tell a story, you can either tell it, or write it down and we read it.'

'Yes.'

'Well, when you do a painting you're expressing something visually. Your picture tells the story. So, it's a visual language. You're speaking to me, telling me something, through the picture.'

'Yes, I see that,' he said considering her explanation.

'But just because artists have the right to free expression, doesn't mean that they have to offend people either.'

'I agree with you, Harry.'

'And what about dipping the cross into his own urine?'

'Well, maybe he could have achieved the same effect by using beer or honey in water or yellow cordial.'

'What do you think Andrea Serrano wanted to say? Do you think he was deliberately trying to upset Christians?'

'I don't really know what his intention was,' she says. 'I can only give you my interpretation. He could have been trying to show the agony of Christ on the cross and how he was soaked in urine and blood. Or maybe, he was aiming at the colours. Only the artist knows that. But once he has displayed his work, it's open to interpretation. And your interpretation is as good as mine.' She stops for a moment. 'But the man's a Catholic, he must have understood the effect his photograph would have on Christians.' Pausing again. 'It did get people talking though. What do you think about it, Harry?

'I think it would have been agonizing on that cross, don't you?'

'That's how they punished people in those days. The Old Testament prophesied that Christ would suffer because of his message and that he would be crucified. Some Jewish leaders blamed him for turning people against Judaism which, was his own religion.'

'Do you think he was?' Harry asked.

'No, I don't,' replied Tully.

'People are always trying to blame others for something, aren't they?... Anyway, I don't like the fact that he gave it the title of 'Piss Christ' and that he used urine over a crucifix because it's offended millions of people. Imagine if someone pissed all over something you loved.' They both laughed.

Harry was very nervous in English the following day when it was time for him to read his speech. He could feel his hands shaking. He walked out to the front desk and turned towards the class, wondering if he would be able to get the words out. He raised his book to just below eye level, took a deep breath and boldly began to read.

'It is my opinion that Andrea Serrano deliberately insulted millions of people with his photograph, "Piss Christ". When I look at a painting, I don't want to feel disrespected. I find it offensive that the artist submerged a crucifix in a container of his own urine and then gave it a very nasty title. Just because he has the right to free expression, does not mean that he has to use that right to offend so many people who love Christ and believe that He is a Holy Figure. Would you like someone to urinate on something you loved?

He looked up shyly to vigorous applause. Even Mrs. Silver was smiling. Harry smiled back.

17

Tully is typing on her laptop at the dining room table, which is where she does most of her writing. Harry is on the floor working on some English homework. The class were learning about different forms of poetry and had to create their own Haiku and Cinquains poems.

Harry had an excellent English teacher. Mrs. Silver discussed and debated current issues with her class and was able to obtain the highest standard from all of her students. She also compiled a book of their best poems.

Tully laughed when she read Harry's poems, thinking they were so charming. He had asked her which one she liked most and she had responded, that she loved them all, she really did.

A cinquain: School

School;
Boring, Tiring.
Writing, Eating, talking
Having no fun indoors
Education.

Haiku: Clouds

Clouds up in the sky
Making cool shapes here
and there
I watch with delight.

Guitar

Strumming little tunes
Soft and as smooth
as the wind
Soothing to the mind

The kettle whistles. Tully stops working. She gets up and makes her way into the kitchen where she pours boiling water into her large grey mug, then swirls a tea bag around in it.

Harry picks up his guitar and begins strumming.

Calling from the kitchen, 'If I'm ever in a coma you should play me that piece you composed in Music. I'm sure it would snap me out of it.'

He laughs.

She returns to the table and resumes her work.

18

'Good morning Tully,' the doctor says. 'What can I do for you?'

'This is the third time I've come to see you for the same reason,' she pauses. 'You know I was referred to you, because you are thought of as a very straight forward doctor.

'Look,' she said, 'My body and face are covered with bruises again and I'm in pain. My back's really sore and I'm finding it difficult to walk.'

The doctor moved forward to examine her. 'Let's see,' he said.

Pointing to her bruises she continues with growing intensity, 'There are big ones all over my legs, my upper and lower back, my arms.'

She waits for a moment while the doctor inspects them.

'There's one on my eye. Look at those huge bruises on my back. That one's immense and it's come back again. This one on my shoulder blade never goes away. It's here in the same spot. How can a bruise just keep on re-bruising itself like that?'

The doctor is honestly shocked. He said, 'Yes, one at a time. They are bad aren't they! How did you get them? Were you in an accident? Did someone beat you up?'

'No, I just wake up with them,' she replied. 'I do feel as though I've been beaten up though. My whole body's aching.'

He then asked her if she was sure that they were not self-inflicted. Surprised at his suggestion, she responded, pointing to her back.

'Of course, they're not self-inflicted. How could I do those?'

'Yes, you're right. It would be pretty difficult to do the ones on your back and shoulder blade.'

He pauses for a moment, trying to find an explanation for the bruising, 'Do you fall out of bed or something?'

'No, I just wake up with them. They would't be as bad as that if I just fell out of bed.'

The doctor sits down at his desk and begins writing his notes. Tully takes a seat opposite him. 'What do you think causes them?'

He considers her question. 'I don't know. Have you ever had any blood tests for spontaneous bruising?'

'Yes, I have and everything's OK,' she replied.

'Well, I can only send you for another test.'

'But what's the point. I've already had the test and everything was fine.'

'Well I don't know what else to suggest,' he said.

'What if your wife or your daughter or mother came to you with these bruises, asking for help, what would you suggest for them? Look closely, some of them are deep, deep bruises, right down there, in the soft tissue.'

The doctor continued writing without raising his head. He looks flushed.

'I wouldn't know what to suggest. I just don't know.'

*

Steven and Peter, were not satisfied with their underhanded games. They wanted to step it up, so they make an overt and fierce attempt to unnerve Tully as she is driving home from the doctor's office. Steven tailgates her and Peter charges up in the right-hand lane very close to her car, his arm raised threateningly. Tully, unmoved retains complete composure.

19

'Oh God, give me a break,' she says, and then, 'GIVE ME A BREAK!' as she enters her lounge room. She drops her keys onto a small dark varnished table and her black shoulder bag next to it. She pulls an exercise book out of the heavy brown bookcase, picks a pen out of her rectangular, grey, incised ceramic container, the first slab pot she ever made as an art student, and one she still loves today. She sits down on the couch and begins to write about her frustrating experience with the doctor.

'And how have you been since last I saw you?' the doctor asks.

'Have a look and make your own assessment...

'But what is this?' she points to one of her bruises.

He looked and blushed. 'I don't know what that is.'

It's a closed shop. Preclusive. Who dares step out of the bounds?

Who dares to step out?

He could see the bruises. He could see the bruises.

Who dares?

'No, I don't know what that is,' he said

Help some. Devastate others.

Who dares step out?

Who's willing to step out of the bounds?
Come on now, step. STEP OUT.
Who's willing?
Who's willing?'

For a few moments Tully remains quiet. Quietly seated. She calmly places her pen inside the exercise book and puts them both down on the couch, stands, heads for the bedroom and SCREAMS.

She returns to the lounge room with her white covered doona, sits down on her pinkish velvety club arm armchair and lifts the doona up over her head, completely covering herself with it. Her voice filters through the stillness and half-light.

Lord God Almighty.
Father of Heaven and Earth.
Hear my prayer.

*

Tully, walked up to the counter at her local Police Station and asks the Police Officer on duty, a young robust, plump lipped, man, with very short, light brown hair and a round freckled face, if she could please speak with someone in private.

'What's it about?' he asks.

'I think someone's been coming into our place when we're not there.'

'Yes, alright, Just a moment. I'll get someone for you.' he replied courteously and without hesitation.

She waited until another policeman came out from behind the window. His countenance was friendly and he looked more mature and more experienced than the officer at the desk: he was taller, thinner, had short brown hair with threads of grey.

He said, 'Come this way, will you?' and directed her down a narrow corridor.

She thanked him and walked down through to the back of the Police station, into a small, unattractive office where, he unrolled his hand in a gesture, indicating that she should sit at his desk, on the chair opposite him. She sat down, not uncomfortably.

'What can I do for you?'

'I think someone's coming into our house when we're not home. And valuable things have gone missing,' she begins formally.

He was extremely polite and asked her if she was reporting a burglary and while he listened with obvious interest, he also studied her very closely as she spoke.

'No, it's more than that,' her reply increasing in rapidity. 'I think someone's hanging around at night as well. I hear noises on my balcony and on the roof. I went out one morning and found the balcony door locks pushed in and a couple of cigarette butts. I don't smoke and nobody else uses that balcony. It's outside my bedroom. When I first looked I saw some damage around the locks. And then I noticed that it has fresh paint around it. It looks like someone's trying to cover their tracks. I've reported it to the police before and they said to ring them when I heard the noises and said that they'd patrol more often at night.'

She paused, taking a breath, in order to compose herself, and said, 'I've woken up with blood on my sheets.'

Then Tully studied his face. 'And, another strange thing happened. The other day I got a message on my mobile from someone named Ang thanking me for the night and apologizing for not leaving me any money. That's the weirdest thing I've ever heard.'

'That could have been a wrong number,' he said

'Yes, it could have. But with everything else going on, was it?'

Disregarding her question, he said. 'Going back a little, did you ring when you heard the noises?'

'Yes, I did. But when the police arrived the scum had already taken off. But I've never seen the Police patrolling. I can't keep on ringing every time I think there's someone out there. I have to protect my child and it would scare him if he saw the police every night. What has to happen to me before I get some kind of help?'

Avoiding her question for the second time he pressed on and asked her if she knew anyone who could have a grudge against her, a boyfriend or someone else? 'No,' she said. She did not. She honestly believed that there was nobody she could have done the slightest thing to, to warrant this.

'Maybe you should think about moving?'

'I can't move again. I've just moved in here.' But in fact, she did end up moving, and a number of times at that.

She pauses. 'I really need help now. I can't deal with this on my own any more. I have a child to protect.'

'The Police can only come out at the time the crime is being committed. We don't have the funds to do it any other way.'

'But this is a crime and it's being committed night after night, after night. Can't you come and take some fingerprints or something? There must be fingerprints. You must be able to do something. Just help me!'

The police officer began organizing his clipboard and moved uncomfortably in his seat. He said, 'The fingerprints have probably gone by now. I'll take down some more details.'

'No!' she said firmly, 'No more details! Just take some action. Aren't you the Police?'

20

And so, after experiencing great trauma, with no available help, neither from the police, doctors or friends, Tully decided not to discuss her predicament with anyone again and so, began the process of separation, compartmentalizing; the good and the horror, the light and the dark.

Allow me to explain the separation a little further. Somehow, she needed to cover her trauma. To cut herself off. Separate from it. She could not carry it around. But even though she divided her life into two sections, split them, her day life, activities, work and family and then the other side, the dark side, she did not wander around oblivious to her predicament. She was still very aware of it. She simply chose to look at life with optimism, move forward. Small step, but steps none the less. Her survival was at stake. She had done everything possible. What were her options? And so, Tully became The Woman. A Woman without an identity.

*

Life's challenges were becoming much more extreme. What the Woman needed was physical practical help. And there was no one to provide it. She needed solid advice and there was no one to give it. In her anguish she, tried to tell one of her old friends, but her friend, having a daughter with schizophrenia and because she thought the Woman's story simply sounded too bizarre, and also, believing that it was the right thing to do, the friend told the Woman's daughter, Rachael, she thought there was something wrong with her mother. And in so doing fractured, for some years, the relationship with the Woman and her child, which up to that point had been so close.

It wasn't until quite some years later, when the Woman apologised, without explanation or defence, unequivocally for her past insensitive comments to Rachael, who had been extremely wounded by them, that they reconnected in a more genuine and loving way.

21

There came a critical point in the Woman's life, when an amalgamation began. A friend, Sally, called in one afternoon, after school with her two children, one of whom attended the same primary school as Rachael. Sally told her, she had been to a Charismatic Prayer meeting and had, miraculously, been healed of Cancer. That prior to the healing, she endured every conventional treatment available. Her doctor was very sorry to say, there was nothing else he could do for her.

Sally said, she filed onto the stage with a number of others who, also sought to be healed with, 'the laying on of hands,' collapsed and woke up on the floor.

When, soon after this experience, Sally visited her doctor he had, in disbelief, told her that she was in remission.

The Woman was fascinated by Sally's story. How could someone lay hands on you and transmit God's healing Power? It was incomprehensible. Many questions ensued and resulted in her friend inviting her to a prayer meeting, the likes of which she had never encountered.

The crowd sang hymns in unison, loudly and enthusiastically, notwithstanding the varying degrees of tonality and tunefulness and prayed together. The healings followed.

The experience was completely foreign to the Woman and her level of discomfort was high. Oddly though, intrigued, she continued to accompany Sally to these meetings and on one occasion, in a hall full to capacity, she heard the words, 'Is there anyone here who has never accepted Jesus into their lives and would like to do so now?'

She does not know what happened, but without warning, her feet walked her out to the front, well before her brain had agreed to it. Afterwards she felt no different. But she could never, have imagined doing anything quite so bold. And then she began to read the Bible.

One might say. 'Why did she do it? I still can't come to terms with it. She's misguided. She's been brainwashed.' Her answer would be, 'I see your point entirely. And I really can't explain it. But that's what happened.'

But the Woman knew that for her, it was the way. The right way. The only way. Because the consequence of that experience, with the Charismatics, had certainly prepared her, given her the grounding, the capacity, had carried her and would prove to be the only real resource, the only artillery she had, for the ultimate victory over the hideous events which tried to fill and dominate her life.

You see, she didn't choose it. It chose her.

But why? Why did she believe in it? Well, she certainly didn't want to. She would rather not have. All the trouble it caused. After all, who was Jesus to her? Some distant figure in history who died on the cross. Someone Jews certainly did not believe in and simply dismissed as just another Prophet.

Whatever had compelled the Woman to take those twenty steps, down the aisle, to the front of the hall? And even after she had, she found the whole thing difficult to come to terms with, grappling with the notion of Jesus in her life, really, for quite some time.

But just one second now, wasn't Jesus Jewish? Weren't all of his disciples, except for Luke, Jewish? Weren't his followers Jewish too? And at the time, they were not called Christians. They were simply another Jewish sect, called, The Way.

So where did her guilt come from, her sense of disloyalty? She thought it came from her belief that Christians later, took Jesus's teaching and made it into something that they wanted it to be. That suited them. And then used it against Jews, senselessly and brutally persecuting them in the name of Christianity. The Woman thought, even Hitler called himself a Christian. How far away from the original teaching could that possibly be? 'Love your neighbour as you love yourself.' It did not say, drug your neighbour. Exterminate your neighbour, rape, degrade, maim, mock or experiment on them. 'Do to others what you want them to do to you.'

But Tully, the Woman can never call herself a Christian. She calls herself a woman who believes in the teaching of Jesus the Christ. The Messiah.

*

It took her years before she was baptized. Initially she did not want to and neither did she think it was necessary. But gradually, she decided, given her dreadful circumstances, that it could be of some value.

She wanted to be baptized by Messianic Jews and finally found a group in Caulfield, Victoria, Australia, to baptize her.

The Rabbi and the lovely woman, she'd been in contact with, who, to mark the occasion, bought her a bunch of exotic, long stemmed flowers, that lived in a narrow, glass vase on the coffee table in her lounge room, for well over a week, possibly two, met her at the local swimming pool and in a ceremony, performed in Hebrew, she was submerged in the shallow end of a chlorinated pool and baptized. She laughed, feeling light, thanked them both and went into the dressing room to change her wet clothes.

22

One morning when Harry was staying with his father, the Woman, positioned at the dining room table was typing on her laptop, writing her feature film.

Steven and Peter, had rented the apartment opposite the Woman. She did not know who they were and was not sure how many hours a day they spent in the place. She'd heard the front door opening and closing quite a bit. But when she was on her way down to the letterbox one morning, she encountered Peter looking smug and self-important, carrying monitors up the stairs into the recently vacated apartment. He smiled at her. Her immediate response was dread. She shuddered. There was something distinctly familiar about him but she could not identify what it was. An odour, look, manner, his lip, the way he bit his lip. Images, vague memories began to filter in. On the way back to her apartment, she kept to the left side of the stairs, avoiding any possible interaction with him.

In their apartment, Steven and Peter sat gawking at their open laptops, scavenging every word the Woman wrote. They have, she does not know how, managed to hack her computer. The Woman's work appears on each of their screens.

'We're in the money,' says Peter, smirking.

'I know,' Steven replies.

*

Late that night, after obtaining and sifting through all of her the material, they begin their research, looking for buyers and the best rates. Who wants it? They write emails and ring around.

TO WHOM IT MAY CONCERN.

The following morning Steven sets out to sell the Woman's work.

He decides to transform his appearance. He certainly does not want anyone to know who he really is. He studies himself in front of the bathroom mirror, deliberating on what kind of look will serve him best. He applies a dark coloured make up. Also applying it to his neck and arms and hands.

He places a short, straight, brown wig onto his head and smooths it down and across his forehead with product. He admires himself, and smiles, pleased with the effect and the forthcoming subterfuge.

He emerged from his apartment in a tannish suit and black-rimmed spectacles, carrying a dark brown, square shoulder bag containing pages of the Woman's stolen film script and some of her stories and made his way to, first stop, a television network. He also has some radio stations in mind.

Later that day an executive, ushers him into his office. They are seated across the desk from each other. The executive looks through the material.

'Looks OK. It could work.'

Steven jots down his credit card details and passes them across the table to the Executive, who says,

'We'll be in touch.'

He smiles and taps the pile of stolen material in front of him. They are both exceedingly pleased with the exchange. They stand and move towards the door. The Executive opens it. They shake hands.

'See you next time.'

'You will.'

23

Tully and her friend and colleague Lily, were power walking along the water's edge at St Kilda beach, arms and legs vigorously moving in unison, both women thoroughly invigorated. Lily began recounting a conversation she had with a mutual friend, Jane, a teacher from Tully's former school, about a boy who committed suicide.

Tully asked who the boy was.

'Angus Bennett,' Lily replies.

'Angus Bennett. That name sounds familiar. I haven't heard anything about it,' Tully said, trying to picture the boy.

'You would have left the school by then.'

'Really, what happened?'

'He was expelled from his last school. He'd only been at the new one for a little while.'

Tully suddenly realized who Angus was. 'Angus Bennett! Oh yes, I remember him.'

'Obviously lots of issues there,' Lily continues.

'Must have been, for him to do that.'

'And they weren't picked up. They're blaming a teacher.'

'A teacher. Why?' Tully asks.

Lily went on to say that the teacher had given the boy a negative conduct report. Stunned, Tully stops. 'You don't commit suicide because a teacher gives you a negative conduct report. You'd have to feel absolute anguish for ages to do something as drastic as that.'

'Of course, I know. But that's what they're saying.'

Dismayed, Tully remembers the conversation she had with Angus when he stood at the desk and read his conduct card. 'Miss if you say that I'll get into really bad trouble at home.'

She says, 'I took Angus for an extra. I signed a conduct card for him and he told me where to go.'

'Lots of teachers would have signed that card.' Lily says reassuringly. It's such a horrible situation. No one ever wants to take responsibility for anything like that. So, they look for someone or something to blame.'

'It's so shocking. I would never want anything I did to contribute to someone else's death.'

They continue walking in silence, until a small white freckled cross breed, off the lead, takes an obvious liking to them and begins bounding alongside. They stop to pat it. Suddenly alerted to his owner's loud whistle, the dog darts off.

'I've been meaning to ask you how you've been going lately.'

Feigning enthusiasm, Tully says, 'Good.'

'Because you haven't been looking too good.'

'I know.'

'It's obvious there's something wrong.'

'Well, what can I do about it?'

'Everyone's been saying stuff to me and I don't know what to tell them.'

'Have they?' Tully asks. 'I don't really want to say anything about it to anyone.'

'Why?'

'Because I don't want them to ask me any questions.'

'So, what if they ask?'

'Then I'll have to say something about it?' Tully said.

'Is that so bad?'

'I'm not sure. It's too much for anyone else to deal with.'

'But you have to deal with it. It's shocking to wake up with blood on your sheets and bruises all over you. And you had that crazy social worker harassing you. I don't know how you cope.'

She said, 'I keep on moving, going, doing and I pray.'

Lily, instantly, puts both arms around Tully and quietly says,

'Do you think He listens?

'Yes, I do,' Tully replies.

'I'll go to the Police with you so you're not alone. I don't know why it didn't register just how bad it was.'

'Thanks.'

24

It was a break from teaching. The Woman took a job delivering food for the St. Kilda council. She was given her instructions and made aware that a particular client would be too weak to open the front door and so the door would be left open for her.

She arrived at the large, red brick, double storey, rooming house with its many old fashion thick, window frames, bag of food in hand and proceeded up the wide gravel path to the front door. However, she was unable to open it. Surprised, she knocked and walked around to the side of the building to see if there was another entrance. There was not. So, she returned to the front. The client had heard the knocking and managed to walk down the passage and open the door for her.

He looked about thirty-five years old, possibly younger. Pale, pale face, even features, extremely thin, with short, shaved, brown hair and was about five foot eight inches tall, though he was slightly bent forward, so was not reaching his full height.

The Woman was hit by his extraordinary peacefulness. She felt completely relaxed in his presence. They both walked down a short passage and into his room. The sense of peace in there was overwhelming. His small room was spotless, ordered and calm. She had never experienced that kind of peace from another person before. The client slowly got back into bed, although he was fully clothed; dark tracksuit pants, a light, clean shirt and brown woollen socks.

The woman placed the food containers, one with vegetable soup and the other two, turkey and a few steamed vegetables, such as cauliflower, carrots and greens and some stewed fruit, on the bench. She went to the fridge, as he had asked her to do, and removed the old food containers, still sealed, from the previous day.

He thanked her, his voice soft, and she said goodbye.

Still reflecting upon her interaction with the client, she took the old food containers to the cluster of empty green rubbish bins out front, in the yard, close to the main road and placed the containers inside one of the bins. Normally, she would have thrown them in, but this time decided not to. They were whisked back out, immediately, by a passer-by. A tidy looking man, in a grey suit.

A few days later, when the Woman asked if she would be delivering to that customer, she was told that he had passed.

*

The Woman drives slowly into the Tyre Factory yard, and pulls up near the entrance. She steps out of her car and is approached by the manager. She tells him that she would like to buy some new tyres and wonders whether the spare needs replacing. He circles her car, examining all of the tyres.

She opens the boot of the car for him and he removes the spare. He checks it and they make their way into the factory, the manager carrying the spare tyre. The Woman is shown a number of different tyres and calculates what she can afford, before finally making her decision. He informs her that the car will be ready in one hour, so she leaves the factory, hoping to find a cafe, for a decent coffee.

One hour later, when she returns to the factory she is met by a young mechanic, swinging her car keys. In lilting tones, he tells her that he is taking her vehicle out for a quick test run. She says, 'Alright.'

He slows to a stop in a narrow side street, just around the corner. Jumps out and slides underneath the car.

He returns to the factory about ten minutes later and as he nears the office door, he directs a short, sharp nod to a man passively waiting there. It is the same man who carried equipment up the stairs, in her apartment block. It is Peter.

Driving home, the Woman becomes aware that in order to reduce the speed of her car, she needs to push the brake pedal right down to the floor. She also notices that the handbrake is loose.

25

She first met Dan when she was an Art student at Royal Institute of Technology. She was twenty years old. It was at a very crowded party, on the first floor in a shared household which, included a school friend, in a large, old, double storey house.

Guests were spilling out of three rooms, on the left-hand side of the staircase, into the passage. The main party room was the first door on the left. She was sitting at the bottom of a very steep flight of stairs, which led up to a bathroom, in the loft. She was in a short, back long-sleeved, crepe A line dress, with three tiny, white crepe covered buttons in the front, long blonde hair, longish, silver filigree earrings, and high wide strapped black shoes, music blaring the Rolling Stones. She had a glass of wine in her hand.

Guests were milling about, struggling to communicate over the resonance.

He stood right in front of her, surrounded by a group of friends from University, her husband to be, included. Dan was also holding a drink, and attempting to converse with her. She liked him. There was so much noise and so the conversation did not get very far. They all moved into the main party room except for her. She remained. He returned.

Tully went overseas about a month after the party. It's possible she saw the group once more prior to her departure.

When she returned to Australia she began seeing her husband. They moved into the back of a bookshop in Elgin Street, Carlton. Sharing it with an acquaintance. It became a focal point for many friends, and countless interesting conversations.

It had an old galley kitchen. There were two bedrooms, up the blue carpeted stairs, on the first floor, a grey brick courtyard, high grey wooden fence, an outside toilet and of course, the laneway out the back. She thoroughly enjoyed living there. It was in that house, that Dan had made an offhand remark about their electric toothbrushes and it was from there, that she and her husband left for England. They had arranged to meet up with another of Dan's friends, who was also a friend of her husbands.

Tully's life with her husband had been an interesting one. They had lived in various places, up north in Queensland, in England, where sometimes she would go for a walk in the late afternoon, very warmly dressed, coat extending to the ground, to meet him at the station, when he was coming home from work at the University in London. Perhaps, they would have an early dinner in a warm Indian restaurant on the way home, interrupting for a short time the feeling of cold, in the freezing English weather.

When they moved back to Melbourne they played with the idea, and in fact, bought the business, 'True Brue' grinding a bean, a coffee substitute, and selling it to health food shops, though it never really took off, the aroma being so intense, it actually killed all the local flies.

They had two children. Both, she and her husband had gone back to study. Her husband already had one degree, and she went back to complete a Fine Art course, going on to teaching and other courses and professions after that. But sadly, when their son was four, the marriage broke down.

Possibly with a bit of work and understanding, if they'd wanted it, their marriage may have continued. No one really knows. Perhaps the respect between them was lost. And when respect goes, there's nothing left. And possibly, if they'd wanted it, and it had survived, she imagined, that he would not have been fat and she would later, not have been raped. But they both thought it was best to part and both had moved on. She'd learnt a lot over the years. Some lessons, she considered, definitely would have been much better to avoid.

So that on every occasion she saw Dan, be it at restaurants, parties or socializing generally, it was always in company.

He was intelligent, interesting, and kind. He always seemed to be writing a movie script but was hesitant about letting anyone read it.

She knew he was a heavy drinker and that, that does not always bring out the best in a person. He had many friends, everybody loved him, and he was well respected at work.

Her ex-husband rang one night to tell her about his death. He was in his sixties and had died at home, from a heart attack. His body was not found until a few days later. She was very upset by the call. Even though she had not seen Dan for a long time, the news had affected her deeply.

The doctor had warned him about his heart and he was trying very hard to stop drinking, had finally completed a feature film script, received funding, and the film was in production. They had started filming in Sydney. It seemed so cruel to her that just when his life was moving in the right direction, his heart ceased to function.

Dan came to her in a dream. She was in the lounge room sitting on the far side of the room on her favorite, deep dusty pink, club arm chair. The light was off.

She wanted to light a candle for him so she went into the kitchen and found two small Hanukkah candles in the cupboard, one unused and the other, slightly melted and bent. She took the good one and some matches into the lounge room. Her tiny Menorah was next to the heater, so she brought it over to the dining room table, fixing the candle into one of the eight small sockets, then lighting it.

It was very quiet and the room was dark except for the flickering candle. She heard soft, muffled, yet very audible voices, completely outside of herself, as if across the room, behind the small burning candle.

'What is she doing?' one of the low voices asked.

'She heard you were dead and lit a candle for you.' It was a familiar voice and she placed it, rightly or wrongly, as the voice of one of his friends who also worked in the film industry. An exceptionally good-looking man, who died of a brain tumor, some years earlier.

Surprised, the first voice said, 'She's crying.'

'Yes, she really liked you.'

Quite close to her now, he said softly, 'Light another one.'

She stood up and went into the kitchen and came back with the second candle. She held the wick next to the glowing flame until it was alight, then melted the bottom and side of the candle, managing to stick the two together. She returned to her chair, sitting there for some time before going to bed.

In the early hours of the morning, she lay listening to a conversation seemingly above her, at the end of her bed.

'They come and do that to her every night.'

'Can't something be done about it?' he demanded.

'No one wants to help her.'

'I want to stay here and help her!'

'I don't know if you'll be able to. We're not allowed to interfere.'

The rest was unclear but the Woman thought, how very sad, it was that it was a dead person, who wanted to help her.

*

That afternoon, she went to see her ninety-year-old mother, in the nursing home where she was a resident. She told her about her ex-husband's friend and how a mutual friend, who her mother remembered, had kept her up to date with his activities. She had actually felt a strong desire to contact him, before his death because she was writing a feature film script and would have liked some-one she knew, and was involved in the industry, to discuss it with.

It was a still and sunny day. The Woman and her mother were sitting outside in a courtyard. She said to her mother, 'I really cared about Dan.' And then, to her astonishment, like a whooshing wind, she heard, 'He really cared about you too.' It was behind her, loud and clear. Unmistakable. Her instinct was to turn around but she did not dare move. It was exactly like the time, just after her father died and she was cleaning up his home in Queensland, she heard her father say, 'You've done a good job.' She did not turn around then either.

*

The next evening, she was cooking in the kitchen. She sensed someone saying, 'If only I'd known. If only I'd known.' She said 'What would you have done if you'd known? Would you have helped me?' He said, 'I couldn't have helped you. I was a drunk.'

And that was all… Or so she thought.

She was ruminating one morning, and said out loud, 'Looks, looks, it's all about looks. Would you have looked at me in the street, if you'd seen me walking past?'

She heard a resounding, 'No. Dressed up, yes. But not like this! But I know you better now and I like you. And I know what happened. So, it's not about looks anymore.' Then…

'Why didn't you ever go for me back then?'

'I was always attracted to you but I couldn't have taken all that drinking and I needed security,' she said.

'I wouldn't have needed to drink. You're so'… It was quiet for a moment, 'calm. That's the first time I've seen you angry.' he said.

It was after a social occasion at her mother's nursing home when, if Tully had not arrived at that moment, her mother would have been paraded around the room, inappropriately dressed.

'I know,' she said. 'Thank you for bothering to come back to see me. And for wanting to stay and help. I won't forget.'

Part Two

26

Harry and Rachael, now adults were choosing their own paths in life and the Woman, Tully, was writing more and more. She had been wrongfully accused of the suicide of a boy and a personal vendetta had been conducted against her, all handled by Steven and Peter.

And while Steven and his wife were still together, Peter's wife, cast him out of their home, when all his underhanded activities came to light, and his children no longer spoke to him. They had always believed him to be a simple, handy man. So, Peter harboured a grudge against the Woman, for what he had been paid to do to her, and consequently, for what his life had become. When he and 'the male' met up and the male asked if Peter would like him to continue the abuse upon the Woman, for which he had his own reasons, Peter had been happy to agree. The male would however, like some monetary reward for this exercise.

The Woman had been in two minds, before making her decision to write about the hidden part of her life. She had considered it very carefully because what it contains is impossible to believe and heartbreaking to write.

Shattering things have happened and are happening to people every single day. There have been wars in many parts of the world, where people have been degraded, treated as less than human, massacred, raped, and murdered. There has been starvation, slavery, child slavery and sexual abuse of every kind. Also, the death of a loved one, which always affects people very deeply.

Each story is different. The Woman's personal account may differ from yours but trauma and torment are trauma and torment, no matter how you look at it.

Every word she says comes from a personal, experiential and observational point of view, with a little research into the behaviour of people with distorted outlooks on life. She has no training or qualifications in psychiatry or psychology or physiology. She has never studied the human mind, so her perspective is not that of a learned or qualified person.

A male and the Woman. Neighbours. There was a short conversation between them. But over time the male became the perpetrator of abuse which, in itself was bad enough but he increased the level of wrong doing slowly and continuously. Drawing others in, building upon the affair. The Woman witnessed friendships formed on the basis of abuse. The male created a circus, enchanting people, leading them into the corral one by one, muzzling them until ultimately the whole phenomenon was so huge and the thing is, nobody cared.

The Woman's first words, when she walked into her brand-new apartment, were, 'I'm scared'. She had made that statement to a friend and his wife who were helping with the move. She hadn't felt fear like that for some time, apprehension, concern, yes, but not actual fear.

There was definitely something about the place. A darkness. Oh, it was nice enough, polished floors, Floor to ceiling windows, plenty of light and a lovely outlook. But she felt a strong sense of foreboding. Still she moved in. Set up. She'd been trying to move on from her past and had taken this apartment to begin anew, a fresh start.

She was standing looking out of her lounge room window, enjoying the view, when she saw the male from her window, in a pale green shirt, looking smart, driving out. She thought, he looks nice.

While working at the loungeroom table, which faced the entire front area of the apartments, leading out into the street, a short time after that, she noticed a pale van pulling up in the driveway outside. A couple of young men piled out and carried four, she noticed, but there may have been more, double mattresses into the apartment below hers.

The following day there were numerous dark-skinned young men, cooking, eating and living downstairs. Roaming about outside, often talking on their mobile phones. There appeared to be so many. Where did they all sleep? she wondered. There seemed to be too many to sleep on four double mattresses.

The cream brick block of apartments must have been built in the fifties. The sound proofing was negligible. The walls were very thin, so that every word came through clearly. It was inevitable that she was going to hear much more than she wanted to. And conversely, they could hear her. Not that she did much talking. Over the phone mostly and to the few people who came into her house.

She knew that they would not have said half the things they did if they thought she could hear. And from their conversation she gleaned that they could somehow see into her apartment.

*

The male and Woman were contrasting types. And if they'd walked past each other in the street, one would never have noticed the other. Completely separate entities passing silently by. But somehow life had thrown them together. She saw it as one of her poor choices. Moving into an unknown area. Somewhere she had never sought to go and it had turned out to her detriment.

'Hello' she said with a friendly smile as she walked into the new apartment block. He looked down at her, surprised.

'Hello,' he answered and turned away.

One of my new neighbours, she thought.

She was unaware however, that he already knew who she was. It would later emerge that two of the Woman's former students, both from different schools, lived in this apartment block. One was already located at the rear of the block and the other moved in with the group of men in the pale van, soon after the Woman. He lived in a free-standing apartment directly opposite her and was partly responsible for later inducting the male into a Game. The three had become friends. All had somehow known and spoken of the Woman's previous predicament.

Another remarkable co-incidence was that the first student was associated with Peter. And, Peter, who together with Steven, years before had caused so much devastation in the Woman's life, lived close by. Peter and the male had formed a friendship.

*

She knew it was possible to get a sense of a person by simply being in their presence. But one can also be wrong. Though in most cases your intuition does tell the truth. Her instinct about the male, did not kick off with the initial hello. It was not a particularly friendly response but neither did she get a bad feeling from it. It was later, when she heard him talking to another neighbour, as if he was instructing her on the art of derision. Also, the way he talked about other people, himself and his activities. Then her instinct yelled at her. Telling her that he could not be trusted, there was something underhanded about him, some underlying menace. She felt that he was working up to something.

She had listened, did not like what she heard but decided not to judge. After a time, she began to warm to him. Heard something in his words which were sensitive, feeling. It could be calming, had a lovely tone and somehow, he'd formed a kind of connection with her. And that connection plus his voice merged into warmth.

*

The male is in his kitchen. He is dressed and ready for work. He woke early, made a pot of tea and buttered some toast. He sits down at the kitchen table where he has positioned his books and notes. He leans over and opens his folder and while having breakfast, he revises his work. He closes the loose folder and takes his dishes over to the sink, washes them and comes back for his folder. The front door clicks, closed behind him. He drives out of the apartment block.

*

He was sitting outside to the left of her large window, in the sun, on a deck chair in skinny, light blue jeans and sneakers, a light open neck shirt and a large rimmed, brown felt hat on his head, reading. It was in the afternoon.

27

The Woman was working at the dining room table as usual and could see the male. It felt calm. Other neighbours, a female and her boyfriend, who lived in an apartment opposite the Woman, arrived home at that moment and after parking their white car, in the allocated parking spot in front of her apartment, meandered over and conversed with the male in subdued tones.

One night, the Woman, comfortably reposing on her couch, listening to soft music, quietly said to herself. 'I wonder why he's not married?'

Next door, the male, long legs outstretched, is lazing in his dark stained Macadam chair.

'I almost got married,' he said, 'I really loved her but it didn't work out.'

Surprised, the Woman said, 'You can hear me.'

'Yes,' he said, 'I can hear. I can even hear your soft breath.'

He paused. 'And you?'

'I was never given another opportunity.'

*

'Say my name,' she heard him say, when they had become better acquainted. 'Say my name.'

'Why?' asked the Woman

'I need it. I need it from you.'

'Why me?'

'It's the way you say it.'

'Asher... Ash.'

28

The Woman was working in the library. The male came in and plonked himself down beside her.

'Hello Tully,' he said, placing a couple of books beside her computer.

'Oh, Hi Asher.' She smiled. 'Do you work here too?'

'Sometimes.'

They began talking quietly. Initially about the library, the computers in the library and the apartment block in which they both lived.

Then, 'Would you like to go to bed with me, Tully?'

'No,' she replied.

'Why not?'

'I hardly know you... How long have you lived is this area?' she asked, changing the subject.

They began discussing various aspects of their lives including the high schools they had attended.

The conversation stopped.

'Let's have one sexual encounter,' he continued.

'No.'

'Just one and then I'll leave you alone.'

'I don't think so.'

'Why, you'll like it, I promise. We'll just do it once then. That's all I want.'

'But you're already sleeping with someone.'

'How do you know?'

'Because when I walked past the apartment opposite me, a female blurted out. 'I've just done him to death. He'll never look at you now.'

*

It was seven o'clock at night. The Woman had already eaten. She heard the male call out. 'What did you have for dinner?' She called back. 'A chop and salad.' He said. 'Then I'll have two chops and a salad.' The Woman laughed. The male laughed. Light heartedly he replied, 'No one has ever laughed at anything I've said before and now suddenly I've become funny.'

The Game

29

The game was firstly, initiated to induct the male into a bizarre situation with the Woman. But it turned into something quite different. Utter depravity.

To understand the game, one has to listen carefully, as with all games, to take note of all the intricacies, the variations, flow and strategies.

The adversary is made to feel important. Made to feel attractive. For the team, if they do not wish to join voluntarily, you must use incentives, Money or other things... So important. Think about your tactics. Begin. Create an interest, then select your allies. Works best with allies whose lives have been boring and monotonous. So easy to do with experience and expertise.

Study your adversaries. Find their weakness. Work your way in. It's like a military operation. Plan. Select your weapons. Then – action. In this case it is, talk, talk, talk.

You must know how and when other players are brought in. How the players pass to one another. Almost like a relay race or a ball game.

The players throw words to each other, gaining momentum, then throw to the one played which, in this case is the Woman. Does she catch, and throw it back, thereby taking part in the game? Or does she ignore, take no action, let the ball, the words, hit her and fall to the ground? Step away. 'I'm not playing. Out!'

The players, if they really want to go in for the kill, must really study their objective. Watch them. Get to know them. What makes them laugh? Listen to their conversations. Use their words. Use their conversations. Throw it all back at them. Make sure they hear the complements you give them. You need to build a rapport. Perhaps encourage them to align to one person or another. But if the complements don't work, then you can change your tactic and begin the insults, degrade them. That may prove to be more effective.

There are also other things you can do in the game. You can temp, encourage the one played, to do something they would not normally do, maybe it's a hidden desire. Then, turn around and hit them with it. Emotional manipulation is another method.

This game is not just a simple matter of who gets to the finish line first. The ultimate goal is entrapment.

For the one played to be victorious, they must keep their eye on their own ball, their own thoughts, their own life. Let the players words drop to the ground, pay no attention to them. You've got your life. It's important. Walk away. Do not get involved.

But how was it that the male initially became so involved in this vicious game? It began with the female, the neighbours, now living upstairs, opposite the Woman, the female and her boyfriend. The female had in the past, been in a relationship with the male. Also, one of the Woman's past students, Jim, who had moved into the apartment block shortly after the Woman, with the men in the light van. He too was involved with the female and her boy-friend, in setting up the game.

They wanted to include the male in their sexual games and hacking schemes. The female had a criminal record and a history of hacking computers. They were aware of the male's success with women, and in their opinion, he was the only one capable of seducing the Woman.

'We're having a bet,' the female's boyfriend said to the male. 'Who is going to be able to seduce the Woman? Do you think you can?... Let's see.' And so, they began... 'We'll talk, find your weakness. It is your prowess. If it's money we'll give you heaps. Fame? We'll get it for you. We'll develop the desire. Increase it. Make it overwhelming. You see, that's how we work, me, the female and Jim. We're smarter than you are. You and your education,' Jim said.

'Where does it get you when we start working on you? When it comes to the art of manipulation, nobody but nobody can out manipulate us. Look at our power. We've got control. We've got You!'

Using reverse psychology, Jim says, 'You won't get her. You won't. You can't.'

'I will if I want to,' the male said, playing into their hands. They had touched on a nerve, his sexual prowess.

'You can't,' Jim continued. 'We could get someone else, really good-looking. Macho. Someone she's really attracted to and she won't be able to resist him. Totally desirable. Strong. They'll do it.' He pauses considering for a moment...'But then again, we've looked for someone like that.' said the boyfriend.

'Really?' the male asked.

'She has to like you.'

The male said, 'Get someone else.'

'We've looked. There is no one else. You're the only one who can get close to her. It has to be you.'

'What did I get myself into?' said the male.

'It's up to you now,' again, the boyfriend.

'We could be sitting on a gold mine.'

Jim said, 'Play her with what happened before, remember what Peter told you.'

'I'll play her. But I won't do that.'

'But we have to hit her up,' the female Interjects. 'She's seen the marks. She knows.'

Consequently, the male agreed to take on the bet. He would be the one to entrap the Woman. He knew how.

*

The female could not have been more jealous of the Woman. She had noticed that on the rare occasion the male allowed himself to be nice, when he let his guard down, he and the Woman had communicated differently.

'Could you love me again?' the female cooed at the male, trying to get him back.

'Yes, if you changed,' he replied.

But in fact, the male descended further and further down and it was he who changed. Going down. Sucked down. Bit by bit. Down he goes. Down, down, to the depths of the bottomless pit.

*

The male told the Woman he was leaving.
She asked him why?
'I don't want to get involved.'
'You don't have to,' she said.
'But it will be better for you.'
'How do you know?
'I can see.'

He was at work when he phoned the Woman. On his way to the cafeteria for a cup of tea. They were talking. He seemed so happy, laughing, cheerful. She thought it was because he was leaving. He'd already asked someone to help him pack up. Earlier in the conversation he'd made a derogatory remark about her and she'd replied in the same flippant, light-hearted, sarcastic way, 'Yes, and I love you too!' Later, she found out, that her comment had been the reason for his good humour.

Subsequently, he felt he was being cut off by her, when in reality, she was simply getting on with her day, her work, her own thoughts.

30

The male calls out to his old girlfriend, the female. 'Oh, the things I do for you. It's really only for you, that I do them. You know that don't you.'

'Hon-nee,' the female says sinking her claws deeper into the male. 'The Woman does not know a thing! That's what we do don't we?' the female cooed, using her phoney, low voice.

'That's our thing. We like to stay home and play people.'

She yells. 'PLAY-A!'

'The male begins, firstly with insults. 'It actually makes me sick. I have to force myself to go in there. I only do it for you, Sugar lips.

'You're losing her. You have to keep on talking,' the female screams. 'Play a! See how long it takes to get her back.'

'She's so smart, so beautiful.' Compliments the male this time. 'Well, used to be.' Back handed complement.

'Everyone said so. And, I love her work. Fell in love with her while reading her work.' The male says.

'You're losing her.' The female yells. 'It looks like she's gone off you... NO... YOU'RE IN!'

'No,' deflated. 'Wait. You're out.'

'It's working! SHE'S LISTENING!'

And that's all they needed. For her to listen. She has to listen or there is no game.

'You're the smart one Hon... eey!' the male tells the female.

'Your IQ is off the charts.'

'I know that honey. And look how beautiful I am. You always play a, I know. Always playing-a. Night and day, its' play, play, play. It's only me you love. Me. Me. Me. I'm beautiful alright, and I'm smart. I run rings around her. And everyone else for that matter. Because I'm so smart. Look at me! I'm gorgeous! You love me. And you always will.'

'Yes always. How could it be any other way.'

'You call me sugar lips remember because my lips are so sweet. Sweet as honey to you? You're mine and don't forget it punk! You have her for a few minutes when she's out cold. Then you have me for hours. HOURS!'

'Oops... you're losing her, losing her... come on lift your game. Faster next time. Faster!

They were consummate players and thought she would be a pushover. They knew every twist and turn; how to talk and what to say. But they found her hard to play. She survived every verbal attack. She refused to play the game. And so later, for him, it became a battle. He needed to win. He was at war. But in fact, there was nothing to win. No prize. No medal. No honour. No protecting a country.

'Don't you have any feelings at all? The Woman once asked the male, from behind the thin wall.

'Yes, I do but I'd like to know what it feels like to be you and I need to gauge your reactions.' the male said.

'And do you?' asked the Woman.

'Yes,' he said.

'All for the game?'

'Yes.'

'Is it worth it?' the Woman asked.

'Yes. We play people like you all the time but you are different and I got to like you. I know that you're the kind of person my emotions would be safe with because you would never betray a confidence. And my emotions are not safe with anyone else. I'm glad I told you. Now I don't have to play you anymore.'

'Don't talk to him. We have to work him'. the female said to the Woman. 'He's a freak with you. Normal with us.'

The male said to the Woman, 'I want you to know who I am.

I used to be, I used to be. I used to be.'

'But are you now?' the Woman asked.

'I used to do. I used to do. I used to do,' he said.

'But do you still?'

31

The male furtively enters the Woman's room. She's been drugged. Half awake, stunned, scared, she says, 'Who are you? What do you want? 'I'm your husband, he says. I've come home late.'

'Oh,' she says softly, stretching both arms out towards him.

He knelt down, his knees on the bed. She drew him down towards her. And onto her chest.

She said, 'You're breathing into me. I can feel every breath.'

'And I feel everything about you,' the male answered.

Once the male sat up on the Woman's bed as she lay there in an ethereal state between consciousness and unconsciousness. She heard soft singing.

'Rest your head, you worry too much...'

They were words from the song she was going to use in the feature film script she was working on. Written and sung by Peter Gabriel.

She heard his soft low voice say, 'I wish I could sing that to you, better.'

*

The male and female came into the Woman's room to feed their appetite for rape. But first the Woman needed to be drugged. Did they spray her with something? Waft something under her nose to make her drowsy and while she was asleep inject her, to make her perform? Did they get substances by pretending to be actors needing to alter their facial features for productions? Were the drugs and substances obtained from the black market? She had no idea but it all seemed possible to her. She did know, however, the effect the drugs and substances had on her.

With the drugs they had tapped into something extraordinary. A small child, ten years old: a beautiful blonde girl, with excellent verbal skills. Trapped, vulnerable, trusting, loving, delicate. Lost. Inside the body of a Woman. 'A delicate soul,' one of her aunts said of her. And from her mother, 'I didn't see that. I saw a strong child. Too strong for me sometimes.'

While in that drugged state, they asked, 'What's your name.'

She gave them her name. A name used only by her parents and close relatives, when she was a young child. They had taken her back in time, to her childhood.

They made that child do things. And did things to her. Things no one should have to endure. Especially a child, unfamiliar with the world. The wickedness. The depravity.

It was, she remembered, at a very early age that she began protecting herself, her emotions, consciously and carefully. She put up a shield.

It was when she was about five that she and her older brother were playing on the swings, in a grassy area along the side of a road, down the street from where they lived. A milk bar on the corner. They had probably just been in to buy a toffee or another kind of sweet, when, they were approached by a thin man in a longish woollen coat. Looking back now, as an adult, of course she can clearly see the gruesome aspects of this encounter.

He invited them to his place which, he said was close by and where he had some sweets for children to eat and toys for them to play with. She had really wanted to go, so young, so trusting. But her brother, said no. He tried to explain things to her but she did not understand and sought to change his mind, encouraged by the long-coated man. But her brother stuck to his guns. He knew. She did not.

It was that young child the male had connected with. The little girl who, must have woken, another night, when he was leaving. She asked, 'Where am I?

He said, 'At home.'

'Who is it?'

'It's your father,' he told her.

'Put the light on Daddy so that it won't be so dark in here,' said the little girl, the one locked in the Woman's psyche.

*

The little girl, was sitting on her bed, both legs tucked under her body. The male was standing next to the bed. They were talking.

He said to the child, 'I'm going away now.'

She asked him why.

'I just have to,' he answered.

She said, 'Why don't you stay? It's beautiful here.'

'I can't,' he said.

'Don't you care about me anymore?' she asked.

'I never did.'

She collapsed onto the floor and cried inconsolably. The male looked down at her and laughed, swung his right leg back slightly and with that leg, pushed her limp body.

*

The male, knew there was something very different about the Woman after he had given her the shot. Something extremely immature, nothing like the adult woman he thought he knew. But he really didn't care. He wanted what he wanted.

What was it that could stop him? His conscience? 'I'll play her, but I won't do that!' he told Jim, his fellow player, when he wanted him to be more brutal in his game. Well, the Woman thought his conscience had been knifed. Had died a slow death, little by little.

He knew the Woman, had experienced extraordinary turmoil in her life, that she was trying to move on from a gruesome situation. When she had been unjustifiably held responsible for the suicide of a boy and Steven and Peter had been paid to harm her. A situation, he said, that, 'if I found myself in something like that, I'd crawl under the bed and hide.'

The Woman's knowledge of the abuse, had been obliterated. The experience can be compared to a patient having an anaesthetic prior to an operation. When the operation is over the patient has no memory of it. There were however, rare occasions when she experienced quick, pyretic spurts, flashing disjointed images, which she instantly rejected as something that could never have happened to her. Though there were, certain signs on her body and in her room.

One would imagine, the Woman, the object of abuse, would wake up feeling contaminated. She did. Her body being physically impacted. The impact making an impression, awake or asleep. Every traumatic experience, every action, every touch and probably every word, which may be consciously blocked is still there, stored in the body's memory system.

32

Initially, it was a sexual encounter, the male sought. Just one he said. One sexual encounter. After that he'd go away. That's all he wanted. One. He promised. She would not agree to it. However later, it emerged that there was much more he wanted.

And so, it was a devastating rape.
The male raped the Woman.
Many knew. Nobody intervened.
Later, she moved. He followed.
It continued with the addition of another.
The female.
Then others.
Many knew.
Nobody intervened.
There was degradation of the worst kind.
Many knew. Nobody intervened.
He admitted it. Called it, even using his name. He wrote about it. Wrote about her. Using her files. Her own writing.
People drawn in to do his bidding.
Many knew.
Some kept their heads down. Others helped him.

Nobody intervened.

They invited him in for coffee, cake.

And... other things. Confided in him. Joked and laughed with him. Played sick games with him. Spoke kindly to him. Included him. Talked to him as if he was just a normal person.

'He is a normal person. Just not with you.'

And nobody intervened.

*

The male, began to watch every aspect of the Woman's life. He put cameras in her home when she went out. He taped it all. Watched it over and over. Tried to dissect it. Pondered over it. Wrote about it for his case study. But still, could not understand her. How did she do that? What made her think that? He quizzed her, hypnotised her. Probed, probed her. Degraded and insulted her. Gossiped endlessly about her. Slandered, played sick games with her but still could not penetrate her being.

He wanted everything from her, inside and out. Every part of her. Everything she did and thought; use her in every conceivable way. To keep her, to give to others. To change who he thought she was. For him it was an attempt to delve into her psyche but for her it was the very, very sick game: all at her expense. 'I know you better than any-one else Tully,' he said. 'I wanted you to fight for me. You would have won.'

He plays. She prays.
Everything he does he does for show.
She's really a very private person believe it or not.
He has a problem with being cut off.
She feels uncomfortable when she is left behind.
For him it is all about power lust and money.
For her it was about getting on with her life.

She'd rather be a real person than live in a pantomime or low rating melodramatic performance.

His emotions surfaced as anger, violence. She could get angry too. Scream and shout when pushed too far. But she was never violent. Never took it out on others. And oddly always saw the other person's point of view. What did he see in her, that made him react so strongly? Something inside himself that he did not want to acknowledge and wanted to destroy? Could that be the reason for his relentless verbal and physical abuse? Is that the reason he wanted to break her? To destroy her. 'She's just so righteous,' he said.

He had spent hours trying to belittle her. Insulted her, tried to drag her down, attempting to put her into a certain emotional space but he wasn't getting the desired result. He called her foul names and discussed various parts of her body to whoever was foolish enough to listen. Taunted her, played sick games on her. He even damaged her furniture. Venom erupted, hatred. What were his motives? Simply power, lust and money?

His involvement grew and grew and in addition to the rapes he progressed into a wild experiment to change the Woman, a perfectly happy healthy, grounded person by bombarding her brain with toxic drugs, which disturb the normal brain function, inducing and producing responses, completely foreign to her. And then, tried to manipulate those responses further, simply to discover what else her brain was capable of doing or how much it could bear. How much the Woman could bear. He was indeed a Scientist.

The Woman didn't think there was anything particularly significant about her brain. She considered it to it be pretty average. She was no great achiever. Didn't particularly perform well at school. But for some, to her unknown, reason, he had decided that her brain was worthy of being studied. So, he put things in place and began his experiment.

She wondered what came first, the experiment or the perversion? Was the experiment devised as an excuse to continue the perversion? Or did the perversion develop as a result of the experiment? She decided that it was the former. The experiment was devised to keep the perversion going. It descended further and further into violence and decadence with the experimenter looking forward to, relishing, his next encounter.

But there was also another experiment. He wanted to see how far he could go before somebody stopped him. He told his entourage, that he would not stop until he was stopped. And nobody would. But when somebody, said 'I'm going to the Police. He said, 'Let's see you try it.' And the female's threatening words were. 'I'll cut you!'

He needed to continue hanging around until the conclusion.

And then, there was a book, the male was writing a book about the Woman. He was writing a book about her, with all the information he's collected. And the book needed to be completed. It needed completing. He needed a good, sound ending for it. A true ending. Something that made her look foolish and weird. So that he could be the smart one. But then it transpired he needed more help, more information, so he enlisted the others, the neighbours.

'What kind of book could that be?' The Woman repeated to herself. 'What kind of book?'

Strangely, she had dreamt an ending. A knifing. She almost stabbed him in the chest but he told her to put the knife down. It was one of her long, intricate dreams. Somewhere in the middle of it she found herself in a large building, running through various rooms, and then outside into the dark yard.

She ran down a long wide staircase. The stairs were black. The female, a dark formless, shadow, was attached to her back. She ripped her off and threw her down the stairs. Continued running, ending in a bare, empty room where there was a tap, and a sink. The door was behind her. She felt him walk past and immediately knew it was him. She did not need to look.

She moved over to the door and stood behind it. She had a knife in her hand. He came into the room. She screamed, 'I hate you!'

He stood in front of her and simply said, 'Put the knife down Tully.'

'There,' she said, throwing it onto the floor. Outside, there was no lush garden.

She realized that there would always be some excuse for him to stay. She knew that while he was using her, making money out of her, he was never going to leave. Finally, they wanted to completely discredit her. Find some way to make her guilty, for their own behaviour.

Was his outrage and hatred really meant for the Woman? Someone he barely, knew? Who had done him no harm. Or was it misdirected? Really anger and resentment towards someone he did know well. From the past. To whom he was unable to reveal his true feelings. Because to the Woman, his behaviour was baffling. It did help a little to understand personality types, when her research led her to the definition of Malignant personalities, psychopaths and sociopaths.

'I hate who you are and what you do,' the Woman told him. She hated how he talked to her and about her. Surprisingly, the male had been really hurt by her comment.

'I'm sorry,' she said.

'You're not sorry.'

'I am.'

'It really breaks my heart when you apologize to me,' he said.

'Every time I got close to you, you pulled away. You probably thought I was playing you and I thought you were playing me. You had no idea how I felt. You probably thought you were having a nice chat.'

'And what happened then?' the Woman asked.

'I turned.'

So, it must have been at that point that his gangly arms and legs began to disappear and his skin cracked, his body becoming a hard, brittle shell. When the Woman needed to turn the male and the female into bird like creatures, no longer being able to countenance their words and actions. No longer seeing them as people. When the warmth she felt turned into revulsion and her brain, which he purported to be so brilliant, began to seize, finding it impossible to believe that she could have been so, so wrong about a person. That anyone could ever treat another living soul like that and especially her.

'Look what you've become,' she said.

'You've lost sight of your humanity. You've become desensitized to what you're doing!'

'You should have loved me like everyone else.' he said.

And little by little.
Bit by bit.
Down he went, down.
Right down.
To the bottomless pit.

For the Woman, to watch the decimation and decay of the male was like watching someone going to bed with Hitler and his evil band. He was seeing the obscenities perpetrated by the female and her boyfriend.

Watching.

Joining in a little.

Then through closed lips expressing a few warm words.

'But I really love that one! That one there.'

Turning.

A slow walk forward... A sigh of resignation... And...

Back to bed with Hitler.

A kiss on the mouth: the one used to curse, lie, betray. Spurt out poison.

'*Frushtick mien herr?*' Breakfast my sir?

33

So, what began with soft words, between the male and the Woman, developed into a demonic, sexually abusive situation, relentless and brutal, with the female, for whom, the Woman heard, the male procured woman, hanging off his arm; working hand in hand to manipulate and control anyone they came into contact with. So that they could continue with their depraved behaviour. In doing so, however, he changed who he was and could have been.

'Don't you have a conscience?' The Woman asked.

'Of course, I don't. Do you think I could do all that if I had a conscience?'

No conscience. No remorse.

'I can do anything I want to you and nobody will stop me. They hate you and love me. After all I'm giving them what they want. And I know how to handle people. You don't.'

He continued, 'I used to be a drug addict and I used to deal drugs so I know how to get things for people. I can get anything you want.'

'Dope? Is it dope? Hard drugs? You name it. I'll get you what you want. I'll help you.

The cycle continues. The played becomes the player.

*

Lying Waiting Plotting.
The treacherous female squawking in his arms.
Lurking.
Attempting to entrap.
Devour.
Bodies poised.
Waiting.
Longing for her warm body.
Longing for night.

The male and the female enter the Woman's room at midnight, armed with a syringe, hair dressing scissors and a large plastic sheet.

'Hit her up,' she orders.

'I said, hit her up! And pausing for a short breath. 'She's a full-on drug addict and doesn't even know it. We keep her stabilised.'

The male sits down on her bed, bends over the Woman and injects her with drugs.

'Listen to my voice.' Attempting to hypnotize the Woman. 'I need you to listen to my voice. I need you to tell me that you love me.'

'No.' The Woman says in her dreams. 'I won't listen to your voice. I don't want to listen to your voice. Use it on someone who wants to.'

The female, to whom the Woman attributed the characteristics of a feathered creature, plumped herself up, took her position on the perch, pecked her feathers, flapped her wings and vengefully, sprayed and hissed.

'Hit her in the head. Go on, hit her in the head, she needs some sense knocked into her. Hit her! I said.'

The Woman stirs. It's vague... she's thinking... Dream?

'I wouldn't love you any other way,' the female says to male.

'You want to do this, you do it for me. You love me, don't you?' And with the scissors, she begins hacking the Woman's hair. 'I just love you when you're bad,' she continues to the male. 'That's the only way I love you.'

Fixing his eyes upon the feathered creature, 'Yes. And I don't love her. Put a bag over her head. And look at what I've got!' he says, still focused on the bird.

'Yes, look at me. I look gorgeous. I just want people to see me.' Spurted the female, 'You've got nothing compared to me. I'm the beautiful one now.' She screams at the Woman. 'You'll never be beautiful again. You look like a drag queen with what we've done to you! I curse you. That's why you never get anywhere. You're just a sl-t to us.'

The male said, 'You won't get very far with her telling her all that! She loves me and I can't stand her.'

'Aren't you glad I made you go and do what you did? You need me to push you sometimes don't you,' the female says.

The male replies, 'Yeah I'm really glad I drug and rape the Woman.'

'I'm scared to go,' the female muttered. 'I won't look beautiful. As long as I'm beautiful, I don't care what I do to her.'

'Really close after that aren't we. Really close. Brings us closer together that. Doesn't it.'

'And,' the female says in her lowest voice, 'People think I'm the crazy one but I'm not. If anyone's crazy it's you. I put on an act to make you look normal.'

'You're not going to tell on us, are you?' the female's phoney syrupy, voice pressed, as she stroked the Woman and told her how beautiful she was, after drugging her into oblivion, raping her together with the male, taking all the fat and tissue out of her face. Using it for their own purposes, their own faces, lips... possibly even selling it. Somehow, twisting her face and injecting her nose with fluid. All done to keep her from looking good, so that no one would look at her. In essence they wanted to change who she was so that the horrific situation could continue.

'She's so righteous. So vulnerable,' the male said. 'I just want to destroy her.'

'How, is it possible,' the Woman thought, when she later saw her face, 'to trust one's feelings and emotions to me,' as the male had said he could, 'and treat me like this?' Devastated, she stares at herself in the mirror.

'She won't tell anyone. God, look at her now. I feel sick,' said the female.

'Why did you take so much?' he asked.

'She was out cold. Why not.'

Clenching, clenching, clenching her claws. 'You've got her now if you want her.'

'She looked better yesterday, didn't she? But we put a stop to that. No one else could do it, could they? But we did it. Peter is so proud of us. He paid us all that money. He finally got what he wanted. Look at that nose! She'll never go out again.'

'But babe you're so, so beautiful. Take my hand. Let's go and make love.'

'We've taken whatever we want. No one will ever catch us. We're too good. We get rid of anything incriminating. Wash everything… and her.' Looking at the Woman's unconscious body, 'She has no clue.'

'You're a prostitute,' she sneered at the Woman, 'only we make all the money. We can do anything we like. That's just what we wanted. We've got the whole crew on board now! All the neighbours.' She laughed.

A beautiful polished facade, covering a putrid, poisonous monster. 'I don't care about her work as much as this' she spluttered.

Satisfied with their savagery, they walk off hand in hand. Into their own room. Into their own bed.

'A very good night.

A very good night.'

The male and female were aware however, that it would be impossible to mistreat the Woman the way they did if they were on an equal footing with her. If she were fully conscious. Not affected by the drugs they administered.

And the onlookers said 'Ho-hum.' And nobody intervened.

34

The Woman, normally rose in the morning bright, cheerful, singing as if nothing had occurred. Had breakfast, showered. Prepared for the day, exercised, shopped, visited the library, wrote. But, she'd woken up this morning with her quilted eiderdown smelling of cigarette smoke and a strange, sweet smell mixed with it.

She got straight out of bed and went into the kitchen. She did not feel good. She found it difficult to walk and her back and anus were very sore. She looked into her night underpants and again, saw blood and discolouration, she saw the sheets, smelt vile odours on her body and in her room.

Usually, she threw her things into the washing machine in the morning but this time she decided to take them to the police station, after she'd rung and confided in Lily.

'Lily, I've woken up smelling of cigarette smoke, male sweat, and a sickly-sweet smell. I'm having trouble walking. My God, my back and anus are so sore. There's blood... And stains on my sheets and undies... And my room... it totally stinks.'

'You've been raped!' she said. 'I'm coming over this afternoon.'

She hung up and hurried to the front door, opened it and examined the lock from both sides. There were no signs of a break in. She carefully inspected all the windows in her apartment. They looked exactly the same. Nothing seemed damaged. She thought 'I'm going to have trouble making a concrete claim.' Then again, she had her stained sheets, pillow slips, underpants, t-shirt and pyjamas and if that was not concrete evidence what else could there be?

She peeled the sheets off her bed and threw them into a large green plastic bag. Ran a bath full of hot, really hot water. And soaked in it. Begging God to wash all the dirt off her.

The smell, the atrocious smell in her room; this time mixed with butter. Death, decay and butter all mixed into one.

She took photos of her things, placed them into a large plastic bag and took them to the police station. She said, 'Look. I need you to look!' She offered her evidence to two Police Officers and began to tell them what she thought had happened.

'Could I be examined by the Police surgeon?' she asked.

'Yes, said one of the Police officers. 'I'll make an appointment for you,' He left the room for a few minutes, then returned. His mind had changed. They also refused to accept her evidence. She wondered why an examination was not going to be provided as she requested? What changed the Officers mind when he returned from dealing with something, someone outside the room? Did he speak to someone? If so, what did they say to him? Did he decide the story was too far-fetched even, with everything she had shown him? It had been extremely difficult for her to do. They should have examined the items for DNA. Was the expense too great? She would have produced all of her photographic evidence as well, bruising on various parts of her body, black eyes, if they had shown the slightest interest.

She picked up her things, put them back into her large green plastic bag and left the police station, feeling sick. They should have completed a basic rape test but her words had fallen upon deaf ears. She left powerless. Who could she go to for help if not the police.

*

Lily arrived at one thirty in the afternoon. She'd taken the afternoon off. She hugged Tully and said, 'Let's go for a walk.' Tully collected her bag, closes the front door and they began walking to the park.

'What did the Police say when you reported, suspected rape?'

'Nothing. They didn't take me seriously. I don't think they believed me.'

'Why?'

'I don't know. Probably because I can't remember what happened. So, I can't say, well he did it, because I didn't see anyone.'

'Were they respectful? Compassionate at least?'

'I felt judged. They were going to let me see the Police surgeon but then changed their minds. The smell in my room was shocking. There would have been DNA. And I showed them everything but they were not the slightest bit interested.'

'How incredibly traumatic for you... You'd think the Police would want to make some inquiries. Someone comes into your home when you're asleep. Rapes you. And nothing is done?

'I don't know how I can prove it, if they won't look at anything I show them. Whoever took unconscionable liberties with my body and life has to be held accountable. They're criminals. Animals!'

'I agree. And I hope they're locked up for good. A person comes to you, anguished, shows you evidence, asks for a medical examination and you're not compassionate, or respectful enough to give their account some credibility. At least do some kind of investigation. What sort of police system do we have? Who do you go to for help?'

*

35

The male lived in the apartment next door to the Woman and every time she saw or heard his car drive past, she sighed with relief. Sometimes she heard him say, 'Going now' or 'Going to score.'

The final time, or so she thought, she lay down on the couch and quietly cried, then sobbed, for an hour. Sobbed out all the anguish, until she was numb. The ordeal was finally over.

She succeeded in getting herself into the kitchen where she cooked some damper, slowly mixing the flour with cold water this time. Giving her a crustier dough.

What does she do when her stalkers, follow her to three separate addresses. What does she do when she's spent more than $11,000 trying to remove herself from them. To rid herself of monsters, without a scruple in the world, who walk around like normal, everyday people drawing others into their web. Tell her. What does she do?

She really needed to relocate. The male knew she had arranged to move into another apartment. He said, 'The female wants me to follow you, Tully.'

The apartment was on the first floor. Quite attractive. Also, in a beautiful area: old, thick trunked, dense, leafy trees on either side of the road, great shopping. She loved it there. It only had one bedroom. The lounge room was large and again had polished floors. The kitchen was well equipped and the bathroom, relatively modern. From her balcony Tully could look across at the garden with its many trees, camellia and rose bushes.

The male and the female, followed her. They moved into the apartment below hers. A few men were already living downstairs and the male either knew them or befriended them, so that they would let him stay.

Soon after, the parents of the man who owned the apartment below, wanted to move in, so the occupants had to leave. The male and the female established themselves in the apartment block next door, where they had during this time, become acquainted with a couple. One of whom the Woman had known since she was a teenager.

The Woman, had seen the male and the female on numerous occasions either walking in the garden, leaning over the balcony next door, which was just across from her bedroom window, or when she was out shopping, or at the local library, where she did a good deal of her writing. She also saw their white, new mobile home which they sometimes parked out in the street. The male's large red, emblemed cap sat on the ledge, in front of the steering wheel. The couple were ever present.

The male stood outside the couple's apartment, begging to be allowed back in. They had stayed with them for a while but had been asked to leave. The couple sat inside. Inside the lounge room. Silent. Wondering what to do. Threatening occasionally to call the police. The male remained zombified outside. He had no followers during those moments. Nobody to manipulate. He had lost his ability to function as a human being. Eventually the couple softened, opening the door. He entered and began to breathe again.

The female remained outside the shot, pulling the strings. Out of view.

The night before she stood outside in the dark, also begging to be let in. Begging anyone who could hear her. She offered them her services, if they would. One man did respond, saying that he would only let her enter. Not the male.

*

The Woman's sick, probably a virus. Dosed up with Panadol. Nose pouring mucus. She wants to drag the television into her bedroom. She puts it onto a carpet, usually kept at the front door. Drags it into the bedroom in a position under the window. Plugs it in. It works. Better than before actually, because the aerial fits more easily into that particular plug.

Lies on her bed, not comfortable, but good enough. The male and the female are next door planning their next move. Their next game. Who to include. How to do it. When. Not put off at all by her state of health.

The other participants in the circus games, the neighbours, those who were aware of the male and female's night time activities, had become addicted to the games. Like alcoholics desperate for a drink or drug addicts hanging out for their next fix. And so, once again the two perpetrators were housed, fed, entertained, and generally looked after. 'He's just perfect,' they said. 'We love him. Those magic hands.'

'Why would we want him to go?'

He was applauded.

'We want you to stay,' their new friend told him.

'We want you to stay.'

His answer was, 'I'll only stay if I can play.'

And so, it was.

The male and female, relished every opportunity to inform the Woman of their intentions and their actions. Seeking at all times her reactions. Looking for a weakness. A crack of some kind. Wanting the Woman to see that they were smart, invincible.

The Woman's life had become quite solitary. Her social interactions and phone conversations at this point, were limited to family, a few friends and advice regarding her work, writing. Boasting to the Woman, the male says, 'You have no idea what we've done to you. We email and ring people pretending to be you. We put on your voice. Publishers, old friends, you name it. Sometimes they tell us to get off the line. They think it's you.' He laughs. 'And my girlfriend, she's brilliant. She sells all your work online, so nobody buys your book. She's got your money. And I've got your name.'

The female laughs. The Woman blocks her ears.

*

After the lease at the second apartment, had expired, the Woman decided to move again. Unfortunately, this time her apartment was tiny. Though it did have an enclosed balcony on which she sat and from where she was able to enjoy the view; the skyline, the red tiled rooves and the brilliant sun sets, through a tall and at dusk, ragged look-ing tree.

Over the months she noticed the colour of the leaves changing from green to apple red, rust, then falling, leav-ing a tall, thin grey outstretched wooden skeleton.

About a week into the move, to her amazement the male and the female appeared. The female had installed herself in the apartment, once again, below the Woman and the male along with the couple they had befriended in the last apartment block, two doors down the street. Her desire was that she would never see them again but there they were.

The Woman had heard the female's deranged, nasty, vulgar talk. She had seen the couple in the street and their car parked in front and at the back of the block. But that was not enough for them. They decided she should see a little more of them.

She was sitting on her balcony drinking a cup of tea, milk and one large sugar, when they drove past very slowly in their large white four-wheel drive. The male driving, the female sitting in the front seat next to him and the previous neighbour, the husband, the one the Woman had known when she was a teenager, leaning forward in the back seat. They were hanging out of the windows which, were wound right down, waving and calling, 'B-y-y e,' and 'We love you...!' The woman, unmoved, watched blankly.

36

The lawyer's reception area was quite luxurious, calming. The Woman sat waiting for him to conclude a conversation. She had spoken to him on the phone prior to attending the meeting and it was he who stated that her situation was one of stalking.

He called her into his office, which, in contrast to the reception area, was quite unexceptional, and offered her a chair on the other side of his desk. He asked to see her licence and Medicare card and photocopied them. Following this, he took some stationery out of a drawer, to jot down notes.

'Do you work?' he asked. She said, 'I used to be a teacher and now I write.'

'What have you written?' he inquired casually. 'Fiction or non-fiction?'

'Non-fiction. About my parents.'

He looked across at her.

'I've also just finished another manuscript.'

What's that about?' he asked.

'All about a Woman's life and how she is raped and the fact that she cannot get anyone to help her.'

He sat down.

She handed him the letter which they had discussed over the phone. One she had previously taken to the Police Station.

He read it quickly then asked her a question. She said, 'I am not going to say anything unless I know that it's an absolute fact.'

He sat down, with his elbows on the desk opposite her, pressing and prodding his forehead and temples rather firmly with his fingers. She watched him as she answered. She said, referring to the letter, 'I have not actually accused anybody of anything.' But he pressed her, saying that she was suggesting who it was. Somehow, she agreed that she was. He said, 'Good enough.'

But it was not actually that she was suggesting who it was. It was the fact that everything she wrote down pointed to the male and female which, is precisely what she should have said.

'Do you have any family?' he asked.

'Yes, I have two children. Both parents.'

He jotted it down.

She said, 'I haven't said anything to them.' His eyes turned back to her. 'Can you imagine telling your son what's happening to his mother?' There was a look of compassion upon his face, and he said, 'Fair enough.'

She described the apartment block in which she had previously lived, referring to it as a village type situation, with apartments on either side of a narrow road, finally leading to the owner's house which was at the end of the long drive.

'Don't you think it would be silly for them to rape you and then follow you?'

She was silent for a moment and then said, 'Well that's a question for them.' She was about to say, 'they're obviously getting something out of it or they wouldn't be doing it.' But she did not.

The meeting was only for twenty minutes and she felt that she had to get all the information out quickly. So, the rapidity of her words increased and volume at which she spoke, became markedly elevated. She said, 'Can you hear me with this mask on?'

'Yes.' he said quietly, 'You're coming across loud,' he paused for a moment, 'and clear.' He said, ' When you write to the Police, you have to state clearly what you are seeking. You are seeking to have these two investigated. Make sure you tell the police what you are seeking. And I think you should neaten up your letter. Put it in point form. If they don't do anything you can go to the Court and get an Intervention Order.'

'I can?'

'Yes you.'

He began rocking back and forth rather precariously on his chair.

'Do you think it would make any difference and what would be the cost, if a Lawyer were to ring the Police about the letter?'

He said either, probably not, or no, I don't think so. 'Make sure you tell the Police what you are seeking. You want them both investigated.'

He got up out of his chair. The twenty minutes had expired.

The letter made no difference to the Police at all.

*

In the middle of the night, the Woman, pulled the white cotton covered doona and pillow slip off her bed and took them into the loungeroom, placing them onto her couch. That was after having overload, listening to the profane, continuous, ranting, the lewd, crude voice of the female downstairs.

Tully had woken, in the morning, on her back. Her throat completely closed, parched. Couldn't close her mouth or swallow. She got herself into the bathroom, turned on the tap, bent over the sink and gulped.

The Woman will not detail the female's entire conversation but let it be said, that the conversations usually related to her expertise on sexual activities and body parts and how she used them, what she did to the Woman and to her work, her hunt for all the Woman's bank accounts and personal information. How she and the male had gone to interview many people from the Woman's past for their book. How they were using her book for their own work. And, as always, declaring their brilliance. As soon as she lay down under the covers, due to her extreme exhaustion, she fell into a deep sleep.

She dreamt there were masses of children in the air, forming gatherings of tight circles, all close together. Some falling. There were flames burning in front of them, but not touching them in any way. Below was a black, hard, scraped, seemingly patterned surface. And darkness.

In the middle of the scraped surface, a circle of light broke through, like a small pool of light, cracking through, from beneath the surface.

In front, slightly to the left, in the darkness, there was a faceless Jewish man in a prayer shawl, his arms outstretched, above him, praying. His breath was fire. His payers so powerful, that they ascended to Heaven as flames.

In the morning, the Woman knew something was wrong. The smell, or rather the intense stench. Disgusting, offensive.

Her body was sore, aching. She felt battered, she felt terror, trauma. She was shaking. She looked in the mirror and saw a twisted face, two black eyes, puffed up. Her hair was cut and her nose huge and completely out of shape.

She looked an absolute mess. She was hit with a sudden attack of fury, and began a bit of ranting of her own.

They had messed up her face, the fat and tissue had been drained from it, leaving dead, hanging skin, so that she would look less than human. It had been ongoing. It made the male think he could do whatever he wanted. After all, now she was just a piece of meat. Her feelings came to the fore.

Each night, she went to bed wondering if she would wake up in the morning. But she did. She turned the radio on. Stood straight. Made her coffee, straining it into a large pink mug, through a dark green plastic coffee filter, buttered her two or three rice cakes.

Sometimes, she got the left-over cake, often chocolate, if there had been a festive occasion the night before, or made some damper, onto which she smothered cream cheese, throwing a few cranberries on top, put it all onto a tray and carried it back into her bedroom, placed the tray onto a narrow wooden chair, from IKEA, which she actually bought for the bathroom.

She got back into bed and had her breakfast, feeling much better after she had finished it.

None of the dirt from the previous night had attached itself to her. But she still felt sick. She heard someone on the radio say: 'If you're pulling on the oars you don't have time to rock the boat.'

It's a great expression which she took to mean, that if you keep your head down, concentrate on what you're doing, what you want to achieve; the outcome, putting all your energy into it, you will not get side tracked. You will not focus your attention on any extraneous factors. Nothing will hold you back from your purpose. Your goal. That's all very well, she did that. But the Woman knew that in her case the boat needed to be forcefully shaken, so that everything underneath rose to the surface.

*

She imagines you're going to say how does anyone ever get into a situation like that? Her answer would be, a few poor choices perhaps. Not considering her behaviour or her words carefully enough. Speaking to the wrong people. Being too friendly. Although, in her opinion, saying hello to a neighbour, cannot be construed as inviting attention to oneself. She is however, more guarded these days.

She has though, learnt from her experiences that you can never assume other people are just like you. That you can speak off the cuff. Consider carefully before you say hello, or anything for that matter, to someone else. And further to that, do not talk about yourself to people with whom you are not close. You don't know who you're talking to.

Sometimes, it takes a lot for a person to learn from their experience. Some people learn easily. Their first mistake and they understand. And then there are others for whom it takes a little longer.

37

The male and the female, prowled into a community bringing out the very worst in the human race. It is amazing, that someone can change people's thinking so that that abnormal behaviour, becomes normal. The Woman witnessed how easy it was for people to give in. A few encouraging words, a bit of money. A few other incentives. Done deal. Synch! She saw it as a disease, spreading through a crop of wheat. In the end, leaving flat, dead earth.

The male and the female spoke openly about their sexual and abusive activities, without shame. He was smooth, sophisticated with words, a convincing talker. Respected, in his day job. It is extraordinary that a community of people can see a Woman, watch as she is blatantly brutalized and not say one word to anyone who could help her. In some cases, join in, in others, simply look away, without a blink of the eye. Walk or drive past and say, 'Oh, what did they do to her today?'

You might ask, 'What kind of mentality could a person who savages others, possibly have? I don't know any monsters like that.' Well perhaps you do. They speak like you. Dress like you. Appear to be just like you. They may be living in the same street. Work with you, frequent the same restaurants. People with responsibilities, pillars of society, or just normal everyday people. But there is something askew and given the right circumstances they will show you another side of themselves which will leave you reeling.

What kind of mentality? A psychologically damaged person. A person who is capable of committing horrendous crimes. And if there were no restraints such as, the fear of discovery or repercussions, their actions would plummet deeper and deeper into deranged debauchery. But they act as though nothing untoward had ever happened. They appear to be good parents, husbands, wives and friends.

Between 1939 to 1945 most of the German Nation were influenced by a brilliant, passionate orator, who turned evil into the new path forward. Abuse and annihilation into a new way of life. Replacing moral values; right for wrong, good for bad, abnormal into normal. Although it is true, that not everyone was affected by the orator. There were those in whom this brutality brought out the best. People opposed to the brilliant orator's ideology and actions. So, you see, that even in the midst of horror, there can always be a glimmer of humanity. And it was that glimmer of humanity the Woman sought.

It is astonishing what a person can be made to do. What Tully could be made to do. Also, astonishing, is that she has absolutely no memory of doing it. How the male and the female, took unprincipled advantage of her vulnerability. She was unable to defend herself in any way. They attempted to throw her onto the scrap heap and then blame her for their own immoral actions. Initially most people were shocked by the male and female's depraved activities, but it developed into an ever-increasing level of acceptance as it had in Nazi Germany.

*

You know it is easy to get lost in the crowd. To hide there. But you also know what you heard and what you saw. Of course, you can rationalize it. Turn it into whatever you want it to be. But the evidence is there. It's clear. Yet you turned your head away. You watched it happening. You did nothing. You could see it happening and often, you joined in. You found it amusing. And when the abusive situation was removed from around people, as it was after the Woman moved residences, those involved were left wondering how they could ever have become embroiled in such a sordid situation. And without any repercussions, they blithely moved along with their own lives as if none of it had ever happened.

Oh, I don't do that anymore,' they might have said. Well great! Good for you. But you did. So, what about all the debris you left behind. Have you made amends for that?

38

The Woman prayed and she prayed. Prayed on her knees, prayed in her head, walking sitting thinking. Why was she in this situation? Why had it been going on for so long? She apologized for anything she could have done to get herself into this hideous situation.

She pleaded with God to make the perpetrators accountable for what they had done, were doing. She thanked Him for all the love and gifts in her life and asked if He could just provide her with more. She wanted Him to part the Red Sea for her, just as He had for Moses and the Jewish Nation, enslaved in Egypt. To part the ocean for her, so that she could reach the other side safely, then close it again, finalizing that hideous part of her life once and for all. At least, send her someone who had her back.

She prayed that someone would step forward with a conscience, remorse, tell the truth. Inform the Police. Back her up. Something concrete, something they would investigate. They would not listen to her, perhaps they would listen, if somebody else told them. Someone who cared enough about the life of another person. She asked God why the police did not want to investigate. She needed physical, practical help. Instead they sent her a case worker.

A case was presented. Imagination declared. Mental disorder insinuated at. A folder created. Let's call it an illness. Interchange fact for symptoms. Medication prescribed to subdue, rendering the target powerless. The abuse will continue but the target will never know. Their capacity to think, has been dulled.

She listened to very convincing Pastors. Pastors she respected. Who made sense to her. Talking about forgiveness and love. Some suggesting, no, saying outright, that there was a reason, a purpose, for someone being in such an incomprehensible situation. Pastors whose sermonized about, believing regardless of your situation. And there were those who said 'May God be with you.' But the letter from James the apostle, said 'Faith without works is dead.' She agreed with that. 'Please don't leave me with just your faith. I need the works associated it. The physical practical help?'

She could not be convinced that she had to go through something so critical, for any purpose. She imagined that these Pastors had not been exposed to such a high level of abuse. No, she thought, surely God did not want her to go through all this.

She went to talk to one of those pastors. A seemingly cheerful fellow. He invited her into his study and she sat down in front, slightly to the right of him. He sat outwards, at his desk, turning towards her.

She explained that hers was a very difficult topic to discuss. He responded by cupping his ear with his right hand, indicating that they were open, and as he said, so was his heart and that he would be listening without any judgement at all.

When she finished saying a little of what she had chosen to tell him of her situation, in the allotted time, he said, he often talked to another woman with a similar story and asked for permission to give her the Woman's phone number. But their conversation never eventuated. Finally, she told him that she'd given up going to the police. He nodded his head in agreement, as good as telling her not to bother, his demeanour reinforced her words.

She left him a couple of her short files, works in progress, which would better enable him to understand her circumstances and who she was. Files which would also lead to this book.

*

The Woman had read many of the Psalms in the Bible and remembered, in particular, part of Psalm 37 which said;

Stop being angry.

Turn away from your rage!

Do not lose your temper.

It only leads to harm.

She knew that was true. But she was overwhelmed with anger. Anger that people could get away with such cruel and mindless crimes. Anger that she was being hurt. Anger, that she had to deal with it all, mainly alone. Anger. Real and unadulterated anger. She felt it in every cell of her body. Was she expected to forgive and even love people who had so brutally invaded her life and damaged her?

Sometimes she burst out verbally and sometimes slammed the door, or maybe slammed an object onto the floor or bench. The consequence of this misplaced release of anger on one occasion, was the shattering of glass on a picture frame and on another, a beautiful crystal jewellery container. Who did that benefit? Not Tully. Although, the outbursts were rare. She did not like losing self-control and often advised herself, when she reached that point of anger, that it would be better not to say a word. Nothing at all. Calm. Keep calm. A punching bag, for instance, would be a far superior option. Physically punching through her anger. And if she had, had a punching bag, it would be getting a great deal of use.

Then she began to bless, as the New Testament teaches, when she really wanted to curse and lash out. Some times were easier than others. She begrudgingly blessed them with her head. Then, mustering enormous effort, tried, with her heart. Though she never let go her desire for justice. She wanted it more than anything else. That and vindication.

She also sang, entirely disregarding the tonal or harmonious qualities in her voice. This also helped. It came naturally to her. Breaking into usually loud song was extremely valuable. She let go then. She knew that if she held onto the overwhelming destructive feeling of anger, she would never get anywhere. It would consume her. And she was not about to let that happen.

Tully was often devastated, by God's lack of action when she really needed Him. Was something alluding her. Was she not listening hard enough? Blocking something? But she thought, He must have been doing something, because every time she was shoved, pushed, kicked down, He took her hand and graciously lifted her back up onto her feet. Until once again, she was standing.

*

Understand the anguish a person experiences in unbearable situations? Parents often miss the intense pain their child feels. And when they suicide, it comes as a complete shock to them. They had not picked up the signs. And the Woman did not understand the full extent of her mother's suffering when she lived at The Nursing Home, until the very end. And of course, later, when she was better able to absorb the situation. Or prior to that, when her mother knew that her mind, her thoughts were becoming a haze. And also, the distress her father clearly endured. And she knew well, that it was possible to conceal one's feelings, when suffering a crisis.

The Woman realizes how difficult it is for people to reach out to those in trouble. Firstly, it's unbelievability. And then, some are simply scared. Others do not want to have their lives disrupted, to rock the boat. But she believes there are those who can help. Will help.

She knew by the reaction of particular people, to whom she tried to relate little bits and pieces of her story, that they could not cope with the details. Usually, she would not get through much of it, realizing that they could not be there for her, that she was better able to cope than they were. So, she changed the subject or simply stopped talking. She also knew how hard it was to believe, as many truths are. Sometimes a lie, well-constructed or even a simple lie is far easier to believe than the truth.

There was a party, she recalls, one afternoon, in a light, open spaced house, with many guests, all familiar to the Woman. Some she'd known all her life. She moved around the large room, which had dividing glass indented, flower pattered, panelled, open doors, one area obviously used for the dining room, the other the loungeroom, speaking to people.

She crossed the room to talk to an older male, standing next to a large window. He was wearing light coloured jeans and a white open neck shirt, soft short brown hair, holding a drink in his right hand. It was in a shimmering crystal glass, the light reflecting onto it from the large, floor to ceiling window.

It had been a couple of years since they'd seen each other. He was the one, at her wedding party, many years before who had wanted to give a speech. It was especially nice of him. He volunteered. It was not prepared. But the

Woman, young as she was, had not encouraged him, so the speech was relatively short.

When the Woman felt comfortable enough, she began relating fragments of her story. He listened, uncomfortable. He said, 'When I saw you come in, I said to myself, here is someone in trouble.' The woman was surprised. 'Do you need any money?' he asked. 'No. No thank you,' she said. 'I'm alright for money.' The conversation concluded and the Woman headed towards the food laden table. She poured herself a glass of fruit juice, with soda water. And wandered back into the company.

*

Eventually, the male began tiring of the entire exercise. He said he wanted out. He may have felt a sudden rush of remorse. Allowed it to rise to the surface. The Woman thought she detected a modicum of decency buried beneath the decay. She wanted to believed him.

He told her, he was sorry for all the abuse he had perpetrated upon her. He said he was going to blow the whole horrendous episode wide open. His and everybody else's involvement in it. The whole thing. On paper. Actually, stand up and give his expose to the world. He would call it, An Experiment Gone Wrong. What in his own experience, people were capable of doing, if they got something out of it. Served their selfish purpose. He said that what he commanded, they did. They followed his command. He made a suggestion, they carried it through. 'How bizarre is that. Who am I?' he said. 'Why do you do what I tell you?' He found it hard to believe the lengths they would go to, simply because he said so.

But oddly, he was still there, still manipulating and conducting the orchestra from backstage.

He decided to turn the game over to the female. She wanted it. Though, he was also losing interest in her; her one track, banal, conversations. And she was a liability. She could not keep her mouth closed and he was moving on to greener pastures. He required a girlfriend, worthy of his intellect, his newly acquired fitness, finesse and recreated face. His big lips, his facelift.

'You should see me now Tully. I'm gorgeous. I can get any woman I want. And look at you. You should see the nose I've given you.'

He wanted the doctor, on level one.

So, he handed the drugged Woman over to the female, in totality. He thought the creature needed someone to play with. Now, he was merely the overseer. She was his proxy. In addition, he knew that it would be the worst thing he could do to the Woman. The most degrading. The most disgusting. That she would feel utter humiliation.

Did the male, have any self-respect? He seemed to have little or no regard for anyone else. Since how was it possible to violate and manipulate others the way he did, if he felt any respect for himself.

He had slept with most of the women living in the apartments surrounding the Woman. 'To get them on side and involved,' he said. 'I do what I have to, to get what I want. With women it's sex. With men. I get them sex.' That, is one way of remaining in control. Obtaining their silence.

He also searched for the Woman, Tully's past friends: school friends, actors,' people she'd worked with, actually, anyone he could find who was or ever had been connected with Tully. He researched them, researched Tully's family. Raved about them, slandered them. He, questioned, probed, slept with some to gain additional information, hopefully inflammatory. A black mark against her, something he could use to bring her down, keep her silent so she would not tell the truth about him.

He used her poignant words, phrases, cut her work up for copy, advertising for networks, radio programs, sold sections, developed work for his lectures. Perhaps his book. Stripped her work, raped it, as he had done her. As he said to his friends, 'She can't do anything to me. Doesn't matter who she tells. I'll always get out of it. I only have to talk to people nicely and they believe me.'

However, he did want the doctor. The Woman was enraged. 'You're a doctor,' she blasted from her kitchen window and you know what he does! How can you do that? Where's your heart?'

'Heart?' She imagined the doctor saying. 'Do I need a heart? Where can I get one of those?'

*

Tully's situation continued relentlessly for years. Taken advantage of by the male who saw her as vulnerable, and his entourage and by Steven and Peter who were paid to mistreat her. They all appeared to be upstanding citizens who were respected in their fields and by their family and friends. Her livelihood had been deceitfully taken from her and her reputation thoroughly tarnished.

One thing on the list of challenges would have been hard to deal with. Extraordinarily, she dealt with all of them, to some extent. There was a life at stake. Her life. And it was important to her. And to those who loved her.

She found her situation extraordinarily difficult to face up to, to deal with and bring out into the open. She had gone through so many emotions, confusion, fear, aggression, distrust, terror, aching and in the end shame, when in a dream she saw herself in an extremely upsetting situation. She also went through different ways of behaving and physical changes.

It's very difficult to imagine people into what you want them to be, or wish they were. So, eventually the Woman began to see the male as he actually was.

39

The traffic was exceedingly heavy along the freeway at eight o'clock in the morning. But Tully, although focussing on her driving, sang uninhibitedly to the car radio.

She drove into the car park of the Secondary College where she had acquired a three-month contract teaching art. She parked her car, looked at herself in the car mirror, straightened her hair, collected her books and her black shoulder bag.

She got out of the car, locked the door and walked hastily through the car park into the school corridors, towards the staff room. She wanted a cup of coffee before she commenced her class and wondered if there was enough time. She stepped into the staffroom. It was crowded, so she decided to go directly to her classroom.

Most of the Woman's students were doing well, working on pointillism, looking at artists such as Seurat as their inspiration. In fact, their work was amazing. Some of it, with the student's permission, she took with her when she left the school, to show as examples to other students.

However, one class had chosen metalwork as their elective, not art. As no teacher could be provided to teach their subject of choice, the students were forced into art.

The Woman found it difficult to spark any interest for her lessons, from these students. So, she suggested to the coordinator that they paint some old chairs, if there were any available. She had been inspired by a magnificently painted kitchen chair, executed by a local artist. It had a low curved back, painted in vibrant colours, using acrylic paint and then lacquered. Her daughter had bought the chair at an auction. She thought the topic would suit this particular class.

As there were not enough chairs, large terracotta urns were purchased instead. Most of the class took to it enthusiastically, using Egyptian vases and motifs as their prototype. The class proved quite successful.

On her way home, on the afternoon she introduced the urn painting class, she thought she would stop for a coffee, in one of the main, cafe filled, shopping strips close to her apartment. She wanted to finish some work while it was still fresh in her mind.

He came into her life unexpectedly. He simply appeared. She'd gone into a cafe desiring a cappuccino, and maybe, if there was one tantalizing enough, a piece of cake, perhaps cheese cake or apple and date.

Hugo was standing at the counter getting his coffee when she walked in. There were not a great many people in the cafe. A few couples and a larger group with two children. One of them looking at an iPhone, his drink on the table in front of him, possibly getting cold if it was a hot chocolate, his attention on the iPhone was so intense. The other, thoroughly enjoying his drink and pastry.

He turned towards the door, perhaps he was expecting someone. He noticed her standing next to him and said he thought he recognised her. It was not a line. She was a little aloof. He invited her to have coffee with him. She said, 'No, I've got a bit of work to do.' She was wary of this kind of meeting and had no intention of having coffee, with a stranger.

She ordered her coffee and sat down at a small table for four, against the wall, on the left-hand side of the cafe. He sat a few tables in front of her, also for four, right next to the window, looking out onto the busy footpath. He drank his coffee while he read a newspaper, looking over at her from time to time. She took out a large note book and blue biro and began writing in her book, while sipping her hot coffee. She did not look in his direction.

*

She had worked quite hard that day and all she wanted to do was loll on the couch and watch television. It was a Tuesday night and she turned onto the SBS movie channel, looked at the synopsis and found it interesting. But it was in Japanese and she would need to go into her bedroom for her long-distance glasses in order to read the subtitles. She was too tired for that. She began looking for something else to watch when her mobile rang. It was Megan, an old friend from her acting days.

After the initial surprise and a very warm conversation, Megan told her that a man named Hugo, had asked for her mobile number. She asked Tully if it was alright to pass it onto him. Tully said, 'Who is he? What sort of a person?' 'Oh, he's a great guy. Really nice. He produces films and is extremely smart.' The Woman hesitantly agreed to give him her phone number.

The phone rang the next night. It was a male voice. After a short conversation she accepted his invitation for coffee. She already knew his name.

*

She was very nervous as she entered the cafe. It was the first time she'd gone out alone with a male, to have coffee, for some time.

He was sitting at a back table, a table for two, in the busy Smith Street cafe, when she arrived. She immediately noticed his lovely face, friendly. Open. Dark hair. Casually and nicely dressed.

He stood up as she approached him and they exchanged pleasantries. They sat down opposite each other. He asked her what she would like to order. She said, 'A Cappuccino please.'

'Is that all?'

'Yes. I had a huge breakfast this morning and I'm not really hungry.'

He ordered two Cappuccinos. There was some small talk about their mutual friend, and then the waiter came to the table with their coffee's. As she sipped her coffee and, in his company, she began to relax. She asked him which part of America he was from. He said, 'New York.'

'How long have you been here?'

'Six months or so.'

He began to explain how he came to be in Australia. He had two sons. One was an animator who lived in Byron Bay and the older son, was a doctor. The older son had gone to Australia first with his Australian wife, who he met while they were both working in a New York hospital. Now they worked in Melbourne.

He went on to talk about his wife who had died of cancer ten years earlier. He adored her. Tully told him how sorry she was to hear that. And then he asked her about her family. She said that she had two children, a girl and a boy and spoke a little about them. He was also interested in knowing what she was writing about. 'Oh,' she said, not wanting to elaborate. 'It's a very difficult topic.' She asked him what he was doing, knowing that he was a Film Producer.

'I've just finished a French comedy. The Writer Director, is a friend of mine. It went really well. The actors were hilarious.'

'What's it about?' she enquired.

'About the crazy relationship between a Professor and his assistant, who hatch a bizarre plan, to steal a mailbag. They wanted to research what people were writing about in their letters because emails are usually the way people communicate these days.' He stops.

Tully said, 'That's a really weird research project. How do they do it?'

'They park their van in the parking lot next to the Post Office so that they can watch the Australia Post driver's routine.

They see him hauling the bag of mail into the back of his van. He unexpectedly goes back into the post office, leaving the van door unlocked, so without any preparation, they decide to make their bold move.

They're a couple of blunderers. They make their crazy heist in full view of a few people. When the driver reaches his destination, he realises that the mailbag is missing, so he begins his own investigation and becomes a sleuth.

Meanwhile the culprits steam open, the letters, making notes and it's a race between the sleuth who discovers who the thieves are and the thieves re-sticking all the letters and returning them to the Post office in the middle of the night.'

'That does sound hilarious.'

'It is pretty funny.'

'I love comedies. Particularly Romantic comedies and Romances like, *You've Got Mail* with Meg Ryan and Tom Hanks' And then she mentions a couple of her favourite films, '*The King's Speech* and *The Book Thief.*'

They found they had much in common and before they knew it, they had been talking for a couple of hours. He had ordered something to eat in the meantime. They decided it would be nice to meet again and he asked her if she would like to go to a party on Friday night. She said she would.

It was about eleven o'clock at night. Tully, met and talked to a number of people at the party. Surprisingly, some of them were people who she had known in the past but had lost contact with, so it was really good to see them again.

She was standing at the fireplace when Hugo came over and put his arm around her shoulder. It was a great party. Crowded. Guests were laughing, talking. There was a fair bit of flirting, drinking and dancing. They began moving to the music. It was a Peter Gabriel song.

'Rest your head...'

There was sense of peace as Tully and Hugo moved to the music, completely at ease in each other's arms.

Tully closes her eyes and relaxed into Hugo's body. They dance.

*

Hugo and Tully were enjoying themselves, walking side by side along the glistening water's edge, on the soft warm sand. The reflection of the sun's bright rays on the rippling pale blue water, compelling Tully to raise her left hand to her forehead, protecting her eyes from the damaging glare, having on that day forgotten her indispensable, tortoise shell, rimmed sunglasses.

Occasionally, they avoided a few sharp clusters of washed up black mussel shells. They were both wearing, jeans and t-shirts. Tully, had on a light yellow, long sleeved one and Hugo's was a short-sleeved black Bonds t-shirt. They were not holding hands.

'I'll race you to that fence,' Hugo suddenly said challenging her. He pointed to an old dark green wooden fence.

'Race me?' she says amused, 'Look at your long legs! They're so much longer than mine. I have to take two steps to your every one.

He smiled at her, 'Yes, but you're much fitter than I am. I can tell. I'll give you a bit of a start.'

She thinks for a moment.

'Come on,' he says.

She says, 'No.' Then, 'Ok!' and suddenly takes off laughing.

Hugo is unprepared for her sudden bolt and runs after her trying to pass. Tully keeps up a good pace. She wins the race. Thrilled, she throws her head back, laughs and strikes a balletic pose. He is surprised by her victory but also impressed. They stand facing each other. She throws her arms around his neck and he wrapped his arms around her and draws her up into the air.

*

Tully and Hugo had been seeing each other for some time. She loved his sense of humour and his ethics. They respected each other. They also liked and respected one another's family. And that was important to Tully.

Tully's elegant, high patent leather heels click uniformly on the pavement next to Hugo's easy strides, their fingers tightly intertwined.

She said, 'I hope the food's good.'

'It is.'

'I wonder what I'll have tonight?'

'Whatever you like,' he says.

'I feel like something deep fried.'

'The calamari's deep fried.'

'I love deep fried calamari.'

After a few moments, Hugo says,

'I'm falling in love with you Tully.'

'That's beautiful,' she says spontaneously.

He says, 'Yeah? How do you feel about me?'

'I'm really attracted to you.' Then more guarded, she says, 'But you don't know my life.'

'I know some of it.'

'Such as?'

'I do know what you're like and I love it when we're together.'

'But there's a lot more.'

'Tell me then.'

'It might change the way you see me.'

'It couldn't.'

She begins telling him her story. He listens closely, without judgement. Somewhere in the telling they have stopped walking.

He has both of his hands around hers.

'Why didn't you tell me this before?'

'I didn't think it was fair and it's not really the sort of thing you go around talking about.'

'Fair to who?'

'To you,' she says and after a moment, 'and I needed to wait until I could trust you.'

He embraces her.

'We'll work it out,' he says gently.

40

She dreamt about a very wealthy and influential couple. They approached her. The wife barely featured. She hung back. But Tully knew she was wearing a very good coat. The husband was a large solid man in a dark brown suit. Brown lustrous, straight hair. Reasonable length. Not long. She didn't see his face clearly or that of his wife but she visualized it as broad and full. Palish. His hair fell across his forehead. Large hands.

For some reason, Tully and other people, who she did not know, were outside a large house. There was some kind of trench around it. She walked across a sort of park, a grassy area with the brown suited man. He had his arm across her back, her waist. He was very friendly towards her. Comforting almost.

Then, with his wife and a few others he ushered the male into a house. Their manner was very friendly, laughing and joking around together. She wondered why.

She didn't see the house then, but she did see the wide passage and felt, that the house was stately. She saw channels of light coming from the large open door. Then, she saw the building. It was dark brown, maybe chocolate coloured, rendered brick and well lit. Shafts of light coming from the windows.

Not long after, they all emerged from the house. The male was wearing a tan leather jacket and had shoulder length, slightly wavy, brown hair. She looked at his face and was somewhat surprised. It was quite unfamiliar to her.

The large man had the male, in some kind of lock behind his back. His head hung forward looking at the ground. He was caught. And nobody seemed to care.

People had been sitting there on the ground, separate, silent, watching. Tully got up and ran after the large man and the male to see what was going to happen to the male but there was no sign of him.

She thought he had been put into a large white van, parked somewhere in the dark. She looked inside the open doors. There were a number of horizontal shelves, compartments in the back, into which people had been slotted. They were lying on slabs under what appeared to be light coloured, folded, rippled butcher's paper, like bread packed into an oven.

They were impossible to see but she knew they were there and that they were alive.

But, where was he? The male.

*

The male sat on the floor taping his numerous boxes. There is an audible burr. He moves all the boxes over and positioned them near the door, ready to be put into his van. Then, he wanders around the apartment tidying, picking things up. He returns to his boxes and stands there, staring at them, hands on his hips.

*

The male and female were driving down a main highway to their country home, after the male had packed all of the boxes into his mobile home, while the female sat on the steps and watched. They had been talking endlessly, to all the neighbours, about their country farm, about its huge, polished floored loungeroom, enormous windows, and wide wooden staircase at the side, leading up to their marvellous bedrooms. The country home, where the male would take on the persona of one of the landed, gentry, smoking his pipe or cigar and she would be the lady of the manor.

They were discussing their brilliance and what they had achieved, how they had fooled all their friends and neighbours, what they had done to the Woman, including taking so much from her and the stupidity of everyone else compared to them. And how on one occasion he stood at the counter in a European bakery, dressed as an old hippie in dark jeans and a long brown wig, using one of his super deep voices, when he saw the Woman enter the shop and looked her way. He did not recognise her at first. She was wearing her mask.

How they'd disguised themselves as father and daughter, him with his artificial stoop, steely grey hair and Fletcher Jones types polyester blend, trousers and crisp white shirt, sitting in cafe's for breakfast, drinking tea and reading the newspaper. And her, with brown straight hair and the obligatory leggings. 'We had so much fun! We're too smart for anyone,' the female squealed with uncontrolled laughter. He turned to look at her, joining in her mirth, when suddenly he lost control of the van, and skidded onto the wrong side of the road, veering into a huge oncoming lorry. Suddenly, the van was silent. Their hilarity ending abruptly, in one horrifying sight.

When the Woman heard about the accident, she thought, things like that only happened in movies. But ironically, they had achieved what they had sought in life. To be anonymous. They were utterly unrecognisable.

Two rotting carcases lying in a plot.

One says,

Get me up.

The other says, I cannot.

41

Tully looks at herself in the full length, plain brown framed, mirror. First, her face. There had been a great deal of damage. But it looked better now. Her skin looked smooth and unlined. She'd put on a light red lipstick. Eyes clear. Her blonde hair had grown back. Smooth. Shiny and well-shaped. She looked at her nicely fitted, to the knee, scooped neck, below the elbow sleeved, soft grey – pink silk dress, turning in each direction. It looked good. She was wearing high black, leather pointy toe shoes and carried a small black shoulder bag. Wore gold hooped earrings and her mother's gold watch, given to Tully well before her mother's death. And now she had a delicate gold wedding band which included a small diamond. She looked good. She was pleased, smiled and left the room.

Tully's husband Hugo, was wearing dark trousers and a white, now open necked shirt. Loose black lustrous hair. She thought, 'Wow, he is gorgeous!'

She had wondered how both families would get along, but was extremely happy with the pervading warmth during the ceremony and celebration; toasts, short enjoyable speeches, laughter and merriment. The celebration itself was quite low key, in a small reception venue. In the distance, they could see the splendid Yarra Ranges. There were rows of grapevines outside and masses of yellow roses in the attractive rose garden. The weather was warm and they were transported by the subtle rose scent coming in through the open window. There were also long patterned glass vases on the table containing the pretty yellow roses. The room was elegant and painted in light, warm tones and the table setting was stunning. The cutlery shone as did the white plates all matching the light decor with light grey carpet underneath the tables. But most of the floor was polished mahogany.

The women look particularly glamorous in stunningly styled, varying coloured clothing. Hair done. The men, handsome, tidy, smart.

Rachael, her husband and two boys, Harry, his wife and their baby boy and Hugo's sons and their families, plus a few close friends, including Lily and her husband were all present. The view, the food; inspired, delicious, shared dishes, creatively cooked meats and fish, vegetarian, intriguing salads, divine imaginative desserts, such as small liqueured tortes and tiny, fruit topped meringues, the white coated, slender, cylindrical two-tiered, wedding cake, thin layers of butter cream throughout and artistically decorated with delicate frosted flowers, flowing down and around the cake and the wine, were all excellent.

*

Hugo opens the car door. He and Tully smile at each other. Finally, Tully had found someone she could love with all her heart. A man who could see beyond what had happened to her. Who could see her, who she was. She gets into the passenger seat. He closes the door and walks around to the other side. The car moves forward. No looking back.

42

Sometime later, when she entered the lecture theatre, nervous about speaking, not knowing how many would be there, it rather surprised her at the number attending. She stood on the podium and began to deliver her paper. The audience were incredulous, quite unprepared for the explicit nature of her talk. For the ordeal she'd suffered. The pain and the brutality.

She said. 'It all began before my son, then aged twelve and I left our family home and went to live in a sunny, two-bedroom apartment. My family, had moved into that very suburb when I was around ten years old and we lived there right up until I was eighteen. The apartment was quite near our old address. Just around the corner actually.'

She told them that she began writing her manuscript in 2003. There was no one to talk to. Nobody wanted any part of it. It was too difficult a subject to handle. People may have thought that fragments of her experience would have a detrimental effect upon their own lives, may rub off in some way. And then of course, there was avoidance and no one to stand by her.

Standing Part Hidden, traces Tully's life, from the time of her marriage break down and move from the family home with her pre-teenage son, to an abused Woman, alone, even when part of a loving family. The title alludes to the reality of shameless abuse and its effects, hidden from general view behind a wall of silence, in a community of seemingly lovely everyday people, beyond the veneer of a beautiful suburb, in a beautiful street, and a desirable life style, while the Woman, functions as an average person in everyday society.

Even years later, when the mindless brutality escalated and many people did know about it, still there was no one to stand up and say, 'This is wrong, unjust. They're cowards. They need to be dealt with.' She said, 'I never sought sympathy. What I wanted was empathy.'

And so, Tully became silent, hidden. She thought it helped her cope with her life, and in many respects it did. But the fact is, horrendous as the nature of the abuse was, it needed to be faced. And the perpetrators needed to be held accountable and not after death, she thought, but while still living.

She said, she laboured for years, needed to understand and earnestly sought, to find the truth in it all. The reasons for having to cross paths with the deceitful, depraved, the thieves. But possibly that, for her, was unattainable and may not be that important after all. She'd spent so much time trying to work it all out. Trying to unearth the real motives. Did it simply come down to the male's statement, 'You should have loved me like everybody else?'

The fact is, some things are unfathomable. They cannot be worked out. Harsh as it is, it happened. And her life was now moving forward.

Epilogue

The Woman searched for more information, more insight into the characteristics of troubled personalities and also for information about women who have been sexually abused in their sleep.

She began reading about Psychopaths, Sociopaths and Malignant personalities which she thought did shed light on her abusers.

A Psychopathy, is defined as a mental (antisocial) disorder in which an individual manifests amoral and antisocial behaviour, shows a lack of ability to love or establish meaningful personal relationships, expresses extreme egocentricity, and demonstrates a failure to learn from experience.

A Sociopath, is similar to a psychopath but they do have a conscience however, it is weak.

Malignant Personalities, fall into the same category as psychopaths and sociopaths but unlike them, their behaviour is masked by a superficial social facade. And they are very dangerous.

Some of the characteristics, attributed to psychopath and sociopaths are: Extreme charm when necessary.

Doctor Sheila Wilson, a Toronto psychologist, who has helped victims of psychopaths says that, 'They play a part so that they can get what they want.' Psychopaths have the ability to manipulate people, have no conscience and their only goal is self-gratification. They have no remorse and no empathy.

Psychopaths and sociopaths also have an exaggerated assessment of their self-worth, lie compulsively and need stimulation. They have poor behaviour control. Promiscuity and gambling are common. They can rape and indulge in sexual acting out, of all sorts. They verbally abuse and perform physical punishments on their victims. Rage and abuse alternating with small expressions of love and approval, confusing and attempting to create hopelessness in their victim. They exploit others and believe that they are all powerful, all knowing, entitled to every wish and have no sense of personal boundaries or concern for their impact on, or safety of others.

Malignant Personalities are extremely dangerous. They are habitual liars. 'They are egotistical to the point of narcissism and believe that they are set apart from the rest of the human race by some special grace.'

They scapegoat, accepting no responsibility for any situation and see every problem as someone else's fault.

They are remorselessly vindictive when hindered or exposed, have no morals, no empathy and are capable of violence.

They break or flout the law, and do not feel remorse or guilt.

Antisocial personalities are defined as people who have three or more of any of above the traits.

The Woman's research into women who have been drugged and raped during their sleep, led to the study by the following women.

Janice Du Mont, EdD, Sheila Macdonald, MN, Nomi Rotbard, MPH, Eriola Asllani BSc, Deidre Bainbridge, BScN, and, Marsha M Cohn, MD, made a study into Drug Facilitated Sexual Assault, [DFSA] a term applied to people who are drugged and sexually violated during their sleep; made to perform sexual acts while unconscious, or under the influence of drugs or alcohol, incapable of giving their consent to a sexual act or resisting the attacker in any way.

It was written in the CMAJ.JAMC Journal, 2009 March 3; 180(5): 513–519. PMCID: PMC2645446 and cited by other articles in PMC.

The study received ethical approval from the research ethics board of Sunnybrook and Women's College Health Sciences Centre and other participating sites.

It found that suspected drug-facilitated sexual assaults were more prevalent than commonly thought and more consideration ought to be given to how best deal with the needs of victims, in these vicious crimes.

In a separate article, there was a case of R V White, 2010, which involved a male and his intimate partner, accused of taking explicit photographs of himself and the partner engaged in sexual activities with a drugged woman. The victim's testimony stated that she had given no prior consent and that the rape, of which she had no memory, was performed while she slept.

Tully's memory of her rapes is non-existent. Although, visible evidence is always present on her body, clothing, sheets, towels and in her home generally.

She went to five doctors and told them of her suspicions. Two of them had sent her off for tests, which did not come up with much. But when she told them her symptoms, it was apparent that they believed her. Her symptoms indicated vaginal and anal rape.

The doctors sent the Tully to specialists, for an ultrasound and a colonoscopy. The colposcope, is a machine that magnifies the actual size the, vagina, cervix, and anus, more than thirty times. It detects cervical and vaginal disease. It detects tears, bruises and abrasions invisible to the naked eye. The examination provides a much more objective and sensitive way of seeing and documenting genital, anal, and other injuries in sexual assault victims.

Tully told the doctors about the rapes, not the specialists. She believes the information regarding the physical violations, was not passed on to the specialists by the doctors, therefore, those undertaking the colonoscopy and ultrasound examinations did not know what to look for, although the colonoscopy did show lesions. Also, Tully realised that the tests, were not conducted within the given time of around seventy-two hours, of being assaulted.

At another time, in another police station, she endeavoured to show a young female Officer her photographs of ongoing bruising on her arms, leg's, eyes and other parts of her body, semen and blood on sheets but sadly only some of the photos were inspected and only superficially inspected, at that.

There are a number of 'date rape' drugs, such as Rohypnol, GHB, also Cocaine and various tranquilizers, used to incapacitate and cause memory loss during and after a rape.

So, obviously the crime can be difficult to report, the victim having no actual memory of the violation. Also, the fact that those drugs, can heighten the level of, or induce an exaggerated sexual response, can make people wonder if the victim was a willing participant in the act. If no drugs had been administered, no artificial reaction could be created.

According to French psychologist Pierre Janet, frightening experiences often, cannot be successfully integrated into the memory, so it can split off from consciousness. The view was later held by Anglo-American psychiatrists.

The section below is quoted from the research carried out by Janice Du Mont, Sheila Macdonald, Nomi Rotbard, Eriola Asllani, Deidre Bainbridge and Marsha M Cohn:

'Using the Delphi method, an advisory committee, which comprised two [2] toxicologists, a forensic biologist, a physician, sexual assault examiner and the program coordinators from seven [7] participating sites, aided in identifying sixteen [16] symptoms that might be associated with suspected drugging. We classified cases of suspected drug-facilitated sexual assault as those in which the person reported a suspicion of having been drugged, in combination with at least one [1] of the sixteen [16] associated symptoms, gave a valid reason for believing that a sexual assault had occurred, and presented within about seventy-two [72] hours of being assaulted.'

The list below; Symptoms for Suspected Sexual Assaults, Tully, had six [6] out of eight [8] for sexual assault and seven [7] out of sixteen [16] symptoms for suspected drugging.

In 1975, The California Medical Association, quoted that rape was 'one of the most psychologically devastating encounters a person can experience.' Symptoms include:

Nightmares, psychosexual distress and other psychological disturbances. Difficulty breathing. Feeling drunk when you have consumed little to no alcohol. Loss of bowel or bladder control. Nausea. Sudden body temperature change that could be signalled by sweating or chattering teeth. Sudden increase in dizziness, disorientation, or blurred vision. **Waking up with no memory, or missing large portions of memories.**

Table 1: Reasons for suspecting drug-facilitated sexual assault

Reason	No. (%) of victims n = 184	
For suspecting sexual assault		
Vague sensation that something is wrong or that something sexual has happened	94	(51.1)
Woke to find clothing in disarray or to find self unclothed	78	(42.4)
Unexplained body fluids (e.g., semen) or foreign materials (e.g., used condom) found on body or nearby	25	(13.6)
Unexplained genital, anal or oral bleeding or bruising	32	(17.4)
Unexplained bodily inquiries (e.g., scratches, bruising)	44	(23.9)
Woke to find uninvited person in bed or in a strange place	43	(23.4)
Reported by witness to have been seen in compromised circumstances	30	(16.3)
Knew that she or he had been sexually assaulted	54	(29.4)
For suspecting drugging		
Total amnesia	115	(62.5)
Partial amnesia	46	(25.0)
Conscious paralysis	12	(6.5)
Loss of consciousness or 'blacked out'	84	(45.7)
Slurred speech	46	(25.0)
Impaired vision	34	(18.5)
Drowsiness	73	(39.7)
Confusion	77	(41.8)
Hangover or symptoms inconsistent with amount of alcohol or drugs used	89	(48.4)
Disinhibition	19	(10.3)
Delirium or hallucinatory state	10	(5.4)
Impaired judgment	31	(16.8)
Dizziness or light-headedness	81	(44.0)
Impaired motor skills	50	(27.2)
Nausea or vomiting	66	(35.9)
Reported by witness to have been seen acting inconsistently with personality and/or amount of alcohol or drugs used	31	(16.8)

('Guidelines', 1975: 420–2). The assumption of extreme trauma even entered manuals for law enforcement. *The New Police Surgeon: A Practical Guide to Clinical Forensic Medicine* (1978), a textbook for policemen dealing with rape victims. Victims of rape can be 'beaten, tied, held by one and raped by another, or viewed by an audience, a typical sequence in a gang rape. It is claimed that almost all rape victims need help dealing with the sense of fear and degradation which so often follows the experience of rape.'

Susan Estrich, an American Lawyer, professor, author, and political commentator noted: [1987]

'Successful prosecution of rape cases, often requires victims to produce evidence of physical injuries to prove that they did not consent. In sexual assault cases, the victim's body is the primary crime scene.'

'THE FORENSIC MEDICAL EXAMINATION IS A CRITICAL PART OF EVIDENCE COLLECTION.'